UFO VS. IRS!

"Laurel and Hardy!" Gnatcatcher screamed.

"What?" the three agents said in unison.

Gnatcatcher did not explain. He roared. "Get me the White House! And get another court order! We're invading the house!"

"The White House, sir?" Smith said faintly.

"No, you imbecile! The house of Agrafan and Netter! Have our men armed, ready to shoot the first sign of resistance! Can you get hold of bazookas?"

Other Tor books
by Philip José Farmer

PHILIP JOSÉ FARMER

RIDERS OF THE PURPLE WAGE

A TOM DOHERTY ASSOCIATES BOOK
NEW YORK

RIDERS OF THE PURPLE WAGE

A Tor Book
Published by Tom Doherty Associates, Inc.
175 Fifth Ave.
New York, N.Y. 10010

TOR® is a register trademark of Tom Doherty Associates, Inc.

Cover art by David Hardy, used by permission of Luserke Agency

ISBN:0-812-51905-1

First Edition: April 1992

Printed in the United States of America

0 9 8 7 6 5 4 3 2 1

CONTENTS

One Down, One to Go

This day, for Charlie Roth, would always be the Day of the Locust.

Twenty-nine years old, a Welfare Department employee, he was now an agent of its new branch, the General Office of Special Restitution. Every workday had been a bad day since he had entered the WD. But in times to come, he would liken today to the destruction wrought in a few hours by the sky-blackening and all-devouring swarms of the desert locust, *Schistocerca gregaria*.

Charlie Roth, attaché case filled with sterilization authorization forms, walked up a staircase in Building 13 of the Newstreet Housing Authority. He was headed toward the apartment of Riches Dott, unmarried mother of many. For the moment, his guilt and tension were gone. His mind was on Laura, the seventh child of Riches Dott. Laura was the only one of the fifteen children for whom he now had any hope. An older brother who had a high IQ and an intense but low ambition was a lifer in Joliet

Penitentiary. An older sister had had a remarkable mathematical talent, long ago whisked away in the smoke of crack and snark.

Advising and aiding Laura was not part of his official mission. But perhaps he could be someone to talk to who really cared about her. He would give her money out of his own shallow pocket if that would make firmer a resolve that must be shaking despite her strong will.

Yet he himself might need help soon. Big help.

Ever since his wife, five months pregnant, had left him, he had been getting more and more easily angered. But their separation was only a lesser part of the steam-hot wrath he could just barely control. The larger part troubled him whether he was sleeping or awake.

His mind was like a water strider. One of those bugs (family Gerridae) that walked on the still waters of ponds. Its specially modified back legs skimmed the surface tension, that single layer of molecules that was a skin on the pond to the strider. The legs of his mind, an arthopod Jesus that had suddenly lost its faith in its powers, were poking now and then through the skin.

"I'm going to sink and then drown! I wanted to save all these wretches because I loved them! Now I hate them!"

Here he was, God help him, a would-be entomologist who could not master chemistry and mathematics. He had given up his goal before he even got his M.A. A man who loves the study of bugs, what does he do when he can't do that?

He becomes a social worker.

As he turned onto the landing, he heard quick-paced footsteps above him. He paused, and Laura Dott appeared. She smiled when she saw him, said, "Hello, Mr. Roth," and clattered down the steps toward him. She was in the uniform of a waitress at a local fast-food restaurant. Just turned eighteen, Laura had been removed from her mother's welfare dependency roll. Though still living with her mother, she was making straight A's in high school and working five days a week from 4:00 P.M. until midnight, minimum wage.

She had always been an honor student. How she could have done that while living in the pressure-cooker pandemonium of her mother's apartment, Charlie did not understand. Equally mysterious was how she had managed to stay unpregnant, drug-free, and sane. Some other youths in this area had done the same, but their mother wasn't Riches.

"Hi, Laura," he said. "I'd like to talk to you."

She went past him, her head turned toward him. She was slim and long-legged, and her skin was as close to black as brown could get. She flashed a beautiful smile with teeth white and regular but long and thick.

"Busy, busy, busy, Mr. Roth. If it's important, see me during my mid-break, eight o'clock. Sorry."

She was gone. Charlie sighed and went on up the steps. At the top he saw Amin Ketcher coming down the hall from the staircase at the opposite end. He reached the door of Mrs. Dott's apartment before Charlie got there, and leaned against the wall by the door.

If he was waiting for Laura, he was too late. Probably held up completing a deal: crack, zoomers, blasters, and snark. The bastard. She's told him time and again to get lost. He's street-smart and shadow-elusive, but a loser: at twenty, the known father of twelve children, boasting of it, yet not giving a penny to support them.

So far he had refused to sign the form authorizing his sterilization. Why should he? He had the cash for a fleet of new cars. Moreover, the ability to knock up a horde of teenagers was, to him, one of the main proofs of his manhood. But they had been pushovers. He wanted Laura Dott because she had only contempt and disgust for him, though she knew better than to insult him verbally.

3

Charlie strode down the hall. "Hey, a Charlie Charlie," Ketcher said. "The General Office of Special Reestituutiion man. The white gooser."

He inclined his handsome copper-colored face to look down on Charlie's six feet from his six feet six inches. His oil-dripping kinky hair was cut in the current "castle" style: high crenellated walls and six-inch-high turrets. A silver-banded plastic nosebone, huge gold earrings, and a ticktacktoe diagram, the symbol of his gang, cut by a razor into each cheek, gave him the barbaric appearance he desired. He wore a sequined purple jacket and jeans overlaid with battery-powered electric lights and neon-tube rock slogans. These flashed on and off while the yang-n-yin music of the EAT SHIT AND LIVE band played from a hundred microphone-buttons on his garments.

The enormous pupils of his glistening black eyes could have been caused by belladonna, used by many youths. But his faint gunpowdery odor told Charlie that he was on snark. The latest designer drug, its effects and chemical traces vanished within five minutes after being used. The narcs had to test a suspect on the spot to get the evidence to convict the user. That was possible only if a van carrying the heavy and intricate test equipment was at once available.

Also, every tiny bag of snark held two easily breakable vials. If the carrier was caught by the police and he had enough time, he threw the bag against anything hard. Bag, snark, and vials went up in a microexplosion. No drug residue was left.

Charlie passed by Ketcher and stopped in front of the door. He could hear the blast of the TV set and the yelling of children through the door. Something crashed loudly, and Riches's high-pitched voice drilled through the plastic.

"I swear, Milton, you knock that chair over again, I slap you sillier'n you already be!"

The doorbell had long been out of order. Charlie knocked hard three times on the door.

"Old fat-ass Riches ain't going to sign," Ketcher said. "You wasting your breath. Or you waiting till Laura come home from school? You wasting your time there, too, Charlie. She ain't interested in no small white dongs."

"You paleolithic atavism!" Charlie said, snarling. "You've been harassing Laura long enough to know she'd sooner screw an ape with diarrhea than you. Anyway, you mush-brained snarker, she isn't going to be around much longer. She'll be getting out of this shithole and away from corpse worms like you. Very, very soon, I promise you."

Ketcher stepped closer to Charlie. His enormous eyes were as empty of intelligence as a wasp's.

"What that mean, paley . . . whatever? You making a racial remark, you blue-eyed shithead? I turn your skinny ass in to the Gooser Office. And what you mean, Laura gonna be gone?"

Charlie regretted losing his cool, and so warning Ketcher that Laura would soon be out of his reach.

The door started to swing open. The TV roared, and the children's voices shrilled like a horde of cicadas.

"You're extinct," Charlie said. "A fly in amber still kicking because you don't know you're dead. Laura'd sooner eat a live cockroach than let you get into her pants."

He stepped through the doorway and closed it while Ketcher yelled, "I'll cut you when you come out, you white motherfucker!"

Sure you'll cut me, Charlie thought. You know I just have to use Riches's phone, and the troops stationed down on the corner will be up here. If they find the knife on you, you go straight to a prison work camp.

Though often in the family room, Charlie had now been admitted only because Riches had not heard his knock. One of the ten children living there had happened to be close to the door. He was optimist enough at the age of six to take the chocolate bar Charlie offered and not wonder what it was going to cost him later. But he slid the bar inside his urine-yellowed jockey shorts, his only garment, before his siblings caught sight of it.

Mrs. Dott answered his greeting with a scowl, and then stared straight at the screen.

Charlie, sighing, pulled three stapled sheets from his attaché case. This visit, he was required only to read to her Paragraph 3 from Form WD-GOSSR C-6392-T. Though he knew that Riches probably could not hear his voice above the blaring commercial or the shouting and screaming children, he did not care.

" ' . . . available to all American citizens (see Paragraph 5 for age, mental, and physical exceptions and restrictions) REGARDLESS OF RACE, GENDER OR RELIGION. Guaranteed free: any new 100% American-made automobile, motorcycle, or pickup truck with 100 gallons of gasoline or diesel oil or alcohol, ten quarts of motor oil, a year's license plate, one year's warranty (see Paragraph 4.d for exceptions) and casualty insurance (see Paragraph 4.e for exceptions and restrictions). . . .' "

Before he could get to the section dealing with the freedom of the government from lawsuits, Riches shrilled, "I told you time and again! Ain't nobody gonna mess around with my body!"

She settled back in the stained, torn, and broken-springed sofa. Riches looks like a huge queen bee swollen with eggs, Charlie thought.

Despite the anger twisting her face, her gaze was fixed on the soap opera unfolding its story as slowly as the wings of a just-molted dragonfly.

Holy humping Jesus! Charlie thought. She's borne sixteen children. Had clap three times. Syph twice. It's a miracle she's escaped AIDS. She doesn't really understand the connection between sexual intercourse and venereal disease, though it's often been explained to her. All those babies have drained the calcium from her bones, spiders sucking out the juice, leaving her toothless and with a widow's hump.

Don't mess around with her body?

Though he wasn't going to change her mind, he had to make his request this final time, then report the failure. The big praying-mantis eyes of Junkers, his boss, would get deadlier and colder. He'd shout, "How you expect this office to keep up its quotas if you piss out on me?"

"Mrs. Dott," Charlie said, "all but six in this building have signed up, and I'm sure most of those will eventually come through. You're forty-five. The cutoff date is forty-six. Why throw all that money away? Chances are high you can't have any more babies, anyway."

Suddenly she looked smug and sly. Patting her anthill stomach, she said, "You think I be too old to have any more? Wrong, Charlie. Got me another. She got one, too."

She pointed at thirteen-year-old Crystal, watching TV.

Her smile became even slier. "The law say Crystal can't sign up with you goosers 'less I say she can till she fifteen. No way!"

She did not look at him as he walked away. Nor did she seem to notice that he was lingering by the door. The dusty wall mirror showed his light red hair and pale and grim face. The dark circles around his eyes looked like Sioux smoke rings signaling for help. His guts hurt as if wasp larvae had hatched inside him and were eating their way out.

Why? What he was doing was rational and humanitarian. It was not just for the good of the people as a whole, though it was that, too. It was also for the good of the people at whom the missions were directed, and it involved no force or cruelty, none that was apparent, anyway.

He saw a cockroach, *Blatta orientalis*, inevitable companion of dirt and colleague of poverty, scuttle out from beneath an end of Riches's sofa. It seized a potato-chip fragment and shot back into the darkness under the sofa.

The piece contained an antifertility drug harmless to humans. Charlie thought that 99.9 percent of the cockroaches might be made infertile. But 0.1 percent would survive because they had mutated to resist the drug. From that would come billions.

He went into the hallway. Ketcher was alone with a youth, an obvious customer. Seeing Charlie, both went down the stairs. A faint acrid odor like battlefield smoke hung in the hall. Charlie felt as if he had gone through a firefight. He was trembling slightly. The hallway with its garbage cans, its dusty light bulbs, and its hot, unmoving air seemed to shift a little. Somewhat dizzy, he leaned against the scabrous, once-green wall for support.

What he was doing was for the best. How many times had he told himself that? The welfare recipients were in an economic-social elevator, its cables cut, falling faster and faster, nothing but disaster at the bottom for them—and for all citizens, since what happens to a part always affects the whole. At the same time, their numbers were increasing geometrically, far out of proportion to the rest of the population. Misery, hopelessness, disease, malnutrition, violence, and deep ignorance were also expanding.

The Ronn-Eagan legislation had not passed without vehement, and even violent, opposition, especially from some religious groups. But the nonreligious reaction to the excesses of the last three decades of the previous century was very strong. And though the law had made already burdensome taxes much heavier, it did promise an eventual lightening of the tax load and a large reduction in the welfare populations. But the vehicle-making, insurance, and petroleum industries, and the businesses dependent on these, were booming.

Someday the welfare problem (which also encompassed a part of the crime-drug problem) would be a small one. Why, then, did he have these dreams in which he strode down a very narrow and twilit hallway with no end? The doors ahead of him were open, but he slammed them shut as he passed.

"Charlie Roth! A ghost among spooks!"

Only Rex Bessey used that greeting. He climbed up from the staircase on which Charlie ascended. His face was a full, dark moon. Then another moon, checked black and white, the vest covering his huge paunch, rose above the steps. He smiled as he limped toward Charlie.

"I got more than today's quota. Those rednecks go apeshit over pickups. How you doing, Charlie?"

"Wasted too much time on Riches Dott, a hopeless case."

"That asshole Junkers thought he was screwing us when he gave me the white area and you the black," Rex said. "But when I remind those Neanderthal rednecks I played tackle for the Bears until I wrecked my leg, they get friendly. That makes me one of the good old boys even if I am a fucking nigger. What helps, I give them a few beers to soften them up."

His attaché case clinked when he shook it.

"Why don't you carry some beer, too?"

"Principles," Charlie said.

Rex laughed loudly. "Sure! You practicing genocide, and you got principles?"

Charlie did not get angry. Once, when drunk, Rex had admitted that he fully agreed with the sterilization policy. He hated his job, but he wouldn't like any work unless it brought in big money.

"This Laura Dott you'd like to rescue," he had once said. "She might make it, but only because she's very smart and strong. What about her brothers and sisters? They were born not so smart or so strong. Why should they have to live in the bottom of the shitpool just because they aren't superhuman? If they were given the environment your average upper-level poor people have . . . well, why go on? We've been through this before. End of lecture. Have another drink?"

Now he said, "Let's hoist a few at Big Pete's."

"The quota."

"That's Junkers's, not the GOOSR's. Why should we sweat and grunt and crap golden turds so that black-assed bastard can get promotion faster? I knew him when he was extorting lunch money from the little kids in sixth grade. He tried that once with me, and I kicked him in the balls. He hates my guts for that, but he isn't going to fire me. He knows I'll tell how he got his job, which he isn't qualified for, and he'll be out on his ass. Forget his quota."

Charlie had heard all this before. He said, "O.K."

Shortly before five, their eyes tending toward the glassy, they walked into the office. Junkers was not there. Charlie faxed his reports and went home to his apartment on High Street. It was one of seven semi-sleazy units in a once-magnificent mansion built by a whiskey baron in 1910. He could look down from his bathroom window at his domain of work, that part of Hell that did not border on the Styx, but on the Illinois River.

The small, dead-aired, and close-pressing apartment rooms rang with his footsteps as if they were great high-ceilinged palace halls. After his wife left him, he had been able to endure the apartment only when he was asleep. Now nightmares swarmed over him like carrion flies.

While his CD player poured out Mahler's *The Song of the Earth*, he ate a TV dinner. Then, sitting on the sofa, staring at the blank set, he slowly drank a tall glassful of medium-priced bourbon. Before he drowsed away, he set the alarm. Its loud ring startled him from—thank God!— a dreamless sleep. Beethoven's *Fifth* was just starting its loud knocking at the door of destiny.

After a shower he looked out the window. The darkness was thick enough that lights were beginning to be turned on. For him, there was only one glow in the Southside of the city: Laura's, a firefly (family Lampyridae) winking above a night-struck meadow.

Twenty minutes later, his hangover only slowly receding, he drove away in his beat-up and run-down car. (Maybe he should get sterilized and have a new car for the first time in his life.) Ten minutes later he was in the Newstreet HPA area. He would not have ventured there alone after dark, but the green-capped Special Police and steel-helmeted Emergency Reserve troops stationed on various street corners ensured a sort of safety. An FDA-unit van passed Charlie on the other side of the street. Black, mournful faces looked out from behind the barred windows.

The shiny new cars were bumper to bumper in the streets, parked on the sidewalks and jammed into open lots between houses.

Charlie's car turned into the alley back of Tchaka's Fast Food Emporium. A young black, his neon-tubed garments glowing, leaned against the wall by the side entrance. When he saw Charlie's car, he shut the door and stepped inside. He was ''Slick'' Ramsey, one of Ketcher's gang. He looked furtive, but that did not mean much down here.

Unable to find a parking space in the alley, Charlie

drove slowly around the block. Before he was halfway, he realized—he jumped as if stung by a bee—that the kids on their work break always stood in the alley, talking and horsing around. But they had not been there.

He brought the car screeching around the corner and into the alley. His headlights spotlighted Ramsey's shiny, sweaty face sticking out from the doorway. Ramsey quickly shut the door. Charlie stopped the car by the door and was out of the car before it had quit rocking. He knew, he just knew, that Ketcher, inflamed with snark, his cool burned away when he found out that Laura would soon be out of his reach, was no longer waiting to get what he just had to have.

Ramsey and another youth caught Charlie by the arms as he burst into the dimly lit hallway. A third, John "Welcome Wagon" Penney, came toward him with a knife in his hand. Charlie screamed and kicked out. His foot slammed into Penney's hand, and the blade dropped. Twisting and turning, stomping on the feet of the two holding him, he broke loose and was down the hall and through the doorway from which Penney had come. Still screaming, he plunged into a large, well-lit storeroom. The workers were huddled in a corner, four of the gang standing guard, holding knives. One worker was down on her knees, vomiting, but several of her fellows were grinning and cheering Ketcher.

At the opposite corner, Laura, naked, was on her back on the floor with Ketcher, fully dressed, on top of her. Charlie saw her face, bloodied, her mouth fallen open like a corpse's, her eyes wide and glazed. Her outspread arms were pinned to the ground by the heavy feet of two gang members.

Silent, all stared at Charlie except Ketcher and Laura. He was savagely biting her nose while pumping away.

Charlie got to Ketcher before the others unfroze. No longer yelling, the others silent, the only sounds the slap of his shoes and those of the pursuers from the hall, he charged. No one got in his way, and he slammed his hands against the pockets of Ketcher's jacket. The vials within the bags broke; the two chemicals mingled; the bags popped like firecrackers; the brief spurts of flame from them looked like flaming gas jets.

Ketcher screamed while struggling to tear off his jacket.

The two standing on Laura's arms jumped at Charlie and grabbed him. Still silent, Charlie slapped at their pockets. There was more popping, and they let loose of him and tried to get rid of the clothes before they burned to death.

The workers ran yelling out of the storeroom. Some of the gang followed them. Two ran at Charlie, their knives waving. By then Ketcher's jacket was on the floor, but he was rolling in agony on the concrete, and seemingly unaware as yet that Charlie was here. Charlie snatched up the smoking and flaming jacket and thrust it into the face of the nearest knife fighter.

He had become a fire in a wind, whirling, slapping jacket pockets, staggering back when a blade went through his left biceps, grabbing a wrist when his cheek was sliced, and twisting the wrist until it cracked. Only because he acted like a crazy man and was as elusive as a gnat did he escape death.

When he saw Ketcher—his ribs, his shoulders, the front of his thighs, and one side of his face bright red with burns, again on top of Laura, but now slamming her head repeatedly into the concrete floor, blood spreading out below her, her mouth slack and open, her eyes shattered glass—Charlie truly became crazy.

Ketcher's only thought now seemed to be to kill Laura. It was as if he blamed her for the burns.

The rest of his gang had run out of the storeroom.

They knew that the cops and the troops would soon be here.

Coughing from the smoke, Charlie ran toward Ketcher and Laura. Suddenly Ketcher sat back. His breath cracked. His chest heaved. But he looked at his work with what seemed to be satisfaction. Where the blood on Laura's face did not conceal it, her deep brown skin was underlayered with gray.

Ketcher rose, and Charlie turned. Ketcher started, and his eyes widened.

"You, you done this?" he said. "The white gooser?"

He half-turned and looked down at Laura.

"The uppity bitch is dead. I had her; she ain't gonna get away."

Charlie stopped and picked up a knife.

Ketcher turned back toward him. "I killed the bitch. I'll kill you, too, Charlie Charlie."

Charlie screamed. According to what he was told, he was still screaming when the cops came. He did not remember.

If he was screaming until his throat was raw for days afterward, it was because he was giving vent to all the futility and despair and suffering and the sense of being imprisoned, straitjacketed, chained, which he felt for himself and which the cesspool dwellers he worked for felt far more keenly than he. And it was for Laura, whose drive and brains might have freed her, given her some freedom, anyway. No one raised here ever really got free of it.

He did not remember stabbing Ketcher many times. Vaguely, he did recall a blurred vision of Ketcher on his back, his arms and legs up in the air and kicking like a dying water beetle. Charlie was told that blood had covered him, Ketcher, and Laura like liquid shrouds. His informant, a black cop, had not been trying to impress him. Born here, she had seen worse when she was in diapers.

When discharged from the mental ward of the hospital five months later, Charlie had no job and did not look for one. In what seemed a short time, he was on welfare.

The irony was doubled when Rex Bessey came to ask him if he wished to sign up for sterilization.

"I'm really embarrassed," Rex said. "But it's my job."

Charlie smiled. "Don't I know. But I'm not going to sign. My wife—you know Blanche—called me yesterday. She just had a baby girl. We're going to get together again. It may not work out, but we're trying for the sake of the baby, for ours, too. I got hope now, Rex. I'm on welfare, but I won't be forever. My situation's different. I wasn't raised on public aid, handicapped by my environment from birth, and I don't have two strikes against me because I'm black. I can make it. I will make it."

Rex got a beer and sat down. He said, "You've been so sunk in hopeless apathy, your friends just gave up. You know I was the last to quit coming around. You just wouldn't stop your dismal talk about Laura. I did my best, but I couldn't cheer you up. I'm sorry, I just couldn't take you anymore."

Charlie waved his hand. "I don't blame you. But I'm better. I know I'll make it. My wife's phone call, well, soon as I hung up, something seemed to turn over. How can I describe it? I'll try. Listen, insects thrive as a species mainly because they breed so wondrously. Kill all but two, and in less than a year, there are 10 billion. It's nature's way; God's, if you prefer. People aren't insects, but nature doesn't seem to care about the individual human or insect being killed, or even millions being wiped out. Laura Dott was one of the unlucky ones, and that's the way it is.

"But I'm human. I do what insects can't do. I care; I

15

hurt; I mourn; I grieve. But I wasn't doing what most humans do. Healing, getting over the hurt as time did its work, accepting this world for what it is. Nor was I trying to do my little bit to make the world just a little better. I gave up even that after Laura died.''

Charlie feel silent until Rex said, ''And?''

''Blanche and I were discussing what to name the baby. Blanche's mother was named Laura, and she wanted to name the baby Laura. I was so struck with the coincidence, I couldn't talk for a minute.''

Rex leaned forward in the chair, his huge hand squeezing the sides of the beer can together.

''You mean?''

''One Laura down, one Laura to go.''

UFO Versus IRS

"They just killed one of our babies!"

· The tiny TV transmitter-receiver orbiting the mothership, *Herschel*, showed the bright side of the craft and, below, the blue-green oblate shape of Uranus. Though *Herschel* was in *epsilon*, the broadest of the planet's eleven rings, the TV viewers on Earth did not see *epsilon*. The coal-black particles composing the ring were too far apart and too small to appear solid at this close range. Nor did the rings cast a shadow on the planet. At this moment and for twenty years to come, Uranus was tipped so that its south pole was to the Sun. When the TV satellite circled to *Herschel*'s other side, its camera would show the bright crescent that the Sun made on the planet's southern hemisphere.

"There's the Sun."

Rees, the anchorman for KPIT-TV, was talking from the Houston studio to his three billion viewers. "That tiny disk of intense light. Not much compared to our bonfire terrestrial Sun, but it's millions of times brighter than the great star Sirius. From Uranus, our Sun is a bright thought in the midst of many pale ones.''

Throughout the special program, the statistics had been spooned to the mass audience because of its limited attention span, an estimated three and a half minutes. The viewers had learned, or a least heard, that Uranus was the seventh planet out from the Sun. It was a far-off celestial body, being nineteen point eighteen times the mean distance of Earth from the Sun. Way out.

The ''jolly green giant,'' as the *Herschel* crew called it, was only one-fifth denser than water and was more massive than fourteen Earths. Its hot core of silicon and iron, however, was not quite as large as Earth's. The outermost layers of its enormous atmosphere were thin, cold hydrogen layers. A spacecraft descending through this (none had) would get warmer as it passed through methane, hydrogen, and helium clouds into a thick fog of ammonia crystals. The warmth was only relative; you certainly couldn't use it to toast your marshmallows.

Below the crystals blowing at hurricane speed would be water vapor clouds. Then the fog would become slush and, later and deeper, hot liquid hydrogen. At a depth of approximately eight thousand kilometers, the temperature would shoot up to more than two thousand degrees Centigrade. Then the spacecraft would penetrate, if it could, a slushy or frozen layer of water and ammonia. The rock-metal core would be at seven thousand degrees Centigrade, hotter than the surface of the Sun.

At this statement, one of the three billion viewers had muttered, though in no terrestrial language, ''A thousand kilometers above the core is hot enough for the third stage of growth.''

Uranus, Rees said, had seven small moons. Puck and Bottom had recently been added to the long-known Ariel, Titania, Oberon, Umbriel, and Miranda.

Like Saturn, Uranus had rings around its equator, but these were not Saturn-bright. They were dark and much narrower, steeped in iron oxides and complex carbon compounds, which absorbed sunlight. These rotated in a thin gas of negatively charged electrons and positively charged ions.

Most of this data had slipped by or been forgotten by most of the viewers. They were absorbed in watching the *Herschel* matching its velocity and proximity with one of the larger objects forming the ring. This was black and about two meters long and three meters at the widest part. Its "body" was flattened out; its "wings" were almost as thick as the body. It looked more like a devilfish or batfish than anything, though it took some imagination to see the parallel. What made it so riveting to the viewers was that it was not the first such object observed. One hundred and thirty-nine had been photographed in this small sector approximately one hundred kilometers wide and ten thousand kilometers long.

"No theory has been advanced, so far," Rees said, "as to why these space objects seem to resemble artifacts. Nor has any scientist theorized why they're so evenly distributed."

"How about the need for living room, space to grow and feed in?" Agrafan said. Agrafan was one of the two viewers in three billion who could have enlightened Rees. Not that he was going to do so.

The *Herschel*, having matched its velocity exactly to that of the object, moved sideways toward it. The screen displayed to the Earthbound audience a closeup so that they could see the four "antennae," two slim spirals of seeming rocklike material projecting from the junction of "wings" and "body" and two pointing from the "belly." The remotely controlled TV machine revolving around the ship showed the cargo bay port swinging out from the hull. Then it showed the brightly illuminated bay and a long mechanical arm unfolding from its base on the hull. Its spidery metal "fingers" were opening.

Netter, one of the two viewers who knew what was happening, said, "About ten seconds to go."

"It's terrible," Agrafan said. "And there's absolutely nothing we can do about it."

Agrafan, the more emotional of the two, discharged a mist of formaldehyde particles, its equivalent of human tears.

The mechanical arm stopped. Its fingers only needed to close to delicately grip the object.

"They can't be blamed," Netter said. "How're they to know?"

"That doesn't help," Agrafan said.

The fingers of the mechanical arm closed on the object. Only two of the three billion viewers were not surprised when the fingers and the object were briefly shrouded in blinding electricity. There was no explosive noise, of course.

The fragments of the object, impelled by the discharge, floated away. The fingers, half-melted, were frozen in their half-grip.

Startled and shocked, Rees cried out a four-letter word as pungent (socially speaking) as the product it referred to. Half of the citizens of the United States heard that, and less than half of that were offended. However, the network executives and millions of members of American religious organizations were outraged.

When the astronauts had recovered from their alarm, the captain explained what had happened. The *epsilon* ring was in a low-density plasma of relatively negatively charged electrons and positively charged ions. Since the electrons were less massive, they moved faster in the ring than the ions did. They collided more often with the rock debris in the ring. Thus, the pieces of debris built up, after a long time, a negative charge.

The astronauts had known this, but the *Herschel*, having been in the ring for thirteen months, had also collected a negative charge. Hence, they had not expected much of a discharge, if any.

The object they had tried to pick up must not have been in the ring long enough to pick up much of a negative charge. That had to be the only explanation possible. The object had been relatively positive to the arm, which, placed on the outside of the hull, had become positively charged.

The astronauts had assumed that the object had been in the plasma of the ring as long as the other space debris. Obviously, it had not. Where, then, had it come from? And when? And why were there so many similar objects that, for some unknown reason, looked as if they had been shaped by sentients?

Neither the astronauts nor the scientists on Earth were ever to advance the theory that the objects were living.

The only two on Earth who could have enlightened the theorizers were too shaken with grief at that moment to pass on their knowledge even if they had wanted to. They were flying—rocketing was a better description—around their huge room deep under a house. They were out of control, bouncing into the frozen carbon dioxide walls and ceiling and floors. Added to their grief were slight injuries from the impacts as their fierce discharges of formaldehyde droplets shot them here and there.

These expressions were matched by anchorman Rees's uncontrollable tears and howlings. Rees was giving vent in his human way to the news that he had just been fired. Moreover, the entire industry would blackball him.

Jeremiah Gnatcatcher, a district director of the Internal Revenue Service, sat behind his desk in the Detroit skyscraper and scowled. The three field agents standing before his desk looked away from his eyes, as cold and as blue-green as Uranus in their human way and shields for a soul as black as Uranus's rings. No one spoke for a long time; if Gnatcatcher had not been grinding his teeth, there would have been complete silence. It sounded to the agents like a shovel digging their graves.

At last, harshly, Gnatcatcher said, "What do you mean, Mr. Agrafan and Mr. Netter can't come here? Since when can any taxpayer refuse to come here?"

Smith, the boldest of the agents, said, "Well, chief, it's this way. Agrafan and Netter have notarized statements by three doctors that health reasons confine them to their house. So, like it or not, we have to go to them. Only . . ."

"Only what?" Gnatcatcher growled.

"Only . . . we can't go to them for the same reason they can't come to us. The doctors say that the allergies and poor immunity-protection systems of the two require them to live practically in quarantine. They're like those babies that live in isolation bubbles."

The three agents could not interpret their boss's peculiar expression. That was because he had not used that particular interplay of facial muscles since becoming district director. It portrayed frustration.

"Okay, okay. So we can't, for the time being, anyway, get them in here to sweat them or go to them for browbeating. What about their lawyers? They don't have any excuse not to come here to represent their clients."

"The firm of Reynard, Wolfgang, Mustela, and Scarab has been very cooperative," Brown, the second agent, said. "After we got a court order to seize their tapes."

"I know that," Gnatcatcher said impatiently. "You dummies never catch on that all my questions are rhetorical."

"Sorry, boss," Smith, Brown, and Jones said in unison.

"So what have our auditors found?"

The three were silent. Finally, Gnatcatcher barked, "What's the matter? You don't *know*!"

"We thought the question was rhetorical," Smith said.

"I'll tell you when they're rhetorical. So, what have they dug up?"

"A can of worms," Smith said. "The tape records look okay on the surface, and they are. I mean, they're not doctored. But still waters run deep. Some of the tapes, most of them, in fact, have codes, references to other companies and record tapes. We had to get a second court order to force the lawyers to explain their meaning."

Smith stopped talking and licked his lips. His eyes were glazed.

"Well?" Gnatcatcher said.

"We uncovered a pyramid of real corporations and dummy corporations, a maze of interlocking financial structures that was so complex that even the computer had to shut down and cool off for a while. Our auditors got dizzy; one of them went to bed with chronic vertigo. But we've uncovered what looks to me like a conspiracy to end all conspiracies, a super-super-conglomerate. The Justice Department is going to have a ball with antitrust suits. If we tell them about this. Personally, I think we should. Anyway, those two hypochondriacs, Agrafan and Netter, if they are only hypochondriacs and not something sinister, make Howard Hughes look like an inept extrovert. They're at the apex of the pyramid and the end of the maze. They own . . . "

Smith licked his lips again. Gnatcatcher said, "Well?"

"Interlocking global conglomerates and several Third World nations worth . . . ah . . . worth . . ."

"Spill it, man! Get it out!"

Smith's voice squeaked.

"Three trillion dollars!"

* * *

"That Walt Whitman knew what the universe was all about," Agrafan said. "Listen.

I celebrate myself and sing myself,

And what I assume you shall assume.

For every atom belonging to me as good as belongs to you.

How about that? An ignorant Earth-person sees intuitively that all is connected. The atoms of Earth's flesh ring from the impact of a meteor falling into Uranus. A temple bell tolls in India, and an entity on Arcturus IV wonders where that vagrant but novel and illuminating thought comes from. Wonderful! Yet, he was an oxygen breather!"

"It's not that simple," Netter said.

They were in the subterranean room beneath the mansion which the local natives had built long ago for them without understanding why or for whom. The locals had been satisfied with the pay, and, if they were curious about it, they had not pursued their nosiness. Nor had the house servants ever tried to find out why their employers never revealed themselves but always gave orders through the telephone. They had been happy with the extremely high pay, though those hired in the beginning had not known that the money was counterfeit. Later, the two agents of UFO, the Uranian Field Operation, had made real money from their investments with the fake.

The house had been built in A.D. 1900 in a suburb of Detroit. Operating from within it, making contact with their servants by telephone and with their business managers by phone and messengers, the two had worked hard for twenty-nine years. It was they who purposely brought about the stock market crash of 1929 and the Great Depression. Unfortunately, the Uranian science-art of calculating trillions of physical factors and trillions of mental vectors had not been as well developed then as it was in the early part of the twenty-first century. The effect of the depression had not been quite what they had calculated. The depression had brought about World War II and, thus, a great step forward in the development and use of rockets. This, in turn, had accelerated and intensified the drive of Earth people to conquer space. Agrafan and Netter would have done better if they had kept Earth's economy prosperous.

Since World War II, the two agents, collaborating with their Uranian colleagues via atomic-impingement waves, had brought event influencing and calculating to a higher level. Or so they hoped. This time, they would certainly set back space exploration for a long time and, hence, destruction of Uranian higher life-forms.

World War II had also caused the invention of the atom bomb much sooner than anticipated. Agrafan and Netter could have started nuclear warfare any time in the last fifty years. They had twelve different ways to bring this about. The danger to Uranus would have been removed forever. That it would also have caused their deaths did not bother Agrafan and Netter. They were willing to sacrifice themselves.

But, though so unhuman-looking and lacking much of the physical and emotional warmth of humans, the Uranians were moral. It was not *right* to destroy the entire life of Earth just to keep themselves from a possible extermination. All things connected, impinged, and transmitted. The ethical mathematics of the universe made such a deed not only a cardinal sin but an ordinal one.

No. The extinction of Earth people was not the way out. The Uranians must just delay the space projects for a long, long time. Above all, they must halt the exploration around Uranus. And this must be done soon. Calculations of all verifiable data showed that the optimum time to complete this phase of their operation was three weeks from now. That delay might mean, probably would, the deaths of the strong-looking but fragile babies orbiting Uranus in the *epsilon* ring. The estimate was a loss of four hundred—if the *Herschel* crew continued pulling in the babies. They probably would. And they would know enough now to trickle-discharge the field on the babies before collecting them. Even so, four hundred babies would die, but that loss would not mean a serious break in the chain of Uranian reproduction and growth.

However, the crew might notice, probably would, the occasional ascent of fiery-tailed egg clusters from the green clouds into space and toward the *epsilon* ring. The *Herschel* might locate and take some of these into the bay. If they did, their examination of the eggs, which looked like small, rough rocks, might—probably would—reveal the embryonic life-forms within them.

Then there would be no stopping the scientists. They would probe the atmosphere of the planet with radar and laser, and the two forms of the adult Uranian, the flying colonies, would be known. What then?

The Uranians' observation at long distance of Earth and the reports of their two agents on Earth had convinced them that war was a deeply established terrestrial cultural trait. It would be a long, long time before the Earth people shucked that trait. The Uranians were willing to wait for that, but until then they wanted to keep Earth people far, far away from them.

Hence, the Uranian Field Operation.

Just now, Agrafan and Netter were watching a TV screen which displayed in infrared. This was connected to a conventional set in another part of the house, the warm part inhabited by the staff of servants and the butler, Goll. Agrafan's remark about Walt Whitman had been evoked by the name of a character, Lance Whitman, in the soap opera *Dinah Stye*. All things connect, impinge, and transmit. One thing leads to another, and then the whole universe is moving.

Another show, *The Signs of the Times*, had followed

the soap opera. Rod de Massas, the host, was saying: "The wave of Aquarius started in 1998. Aquarius, as we know, is the sign of dreams and aspirations of betterment and ideals. So far, there seems to have been little of this because of the worldwide wars, revolutions, and violent agitation for social, political, and economic reform. These, however, have been motivated by idealism, the fierce desire to make changes for the better.

"Also, as I predicted in 1998—the stars never lie—the first fourteen years of Aquarius were still influenced by Capricorn. But that pernicious influence is a dying wave. The age of Aquarius is beginning to bloom. It will flourish as it never has before, will be far stronger now than at any time in the past. The world will begin its march toward Utopia. The Neptune factor will have ebbed to silence, and the times will be controlled by the ruler of Aquarius, the planet Uranus."

"Half-right, half-wrong," Netter said.

"Mostly wrong, but he should be honored for the tiny fraction of right," Agrafan said.

Even in "empty" space, particles and radiation impinged on each other, resonated, bumped, and penetrated. The universe was crammed with shocks, small and big; everything affected everything else. Some things were, from the sentient viewpoint, more influential than others. Size, location, distance, and velocity of inanimate things and animate beings determined what was most influential. There were also the factors of weak and strong linkage and of intent.

Intent, of course, was possible only for animate beings, except the star Sirius and a rather far-off galaxy.

The Uranians knew that the total interconnectedness of all matter was a fact. But it was and probably always would be impossible to know the size, location, and velocity of every bit of matter in the universe. The data they could get about the solar system was a mere microfraction of what was needed for even gross influencing. Nevertheless, on Earth, the two agents had had considerable success in predicting and influencing on a rather gross level. It was, however, their ignorance on a fine-grain level that now threatened their plans. They did not know that Gnatcatcher had been suffering for a long time from a duodenal ulcer.

They could not be blamed for this. Gnatcatcher had not told anybody about it because he was obsessed with his power as district IRS director. If he went to the hospital for tests and, probably, for surgery, his assistant would take over his directorship. Gnatcatcher would be powerless for a long time. And who knew what machinations his assistant might resort to in order to oust his boss?

The increasing pain from the ulcer was, however, making him behave less cautiously than he should, not to mention less legally. The news about the secret global business empire of Agrafan and Netter and the suspicion that they might be—must be—cheating the IRS made his ulcer flare up like a sunspot and his anger explode like a nova.

"Get everybody and every machine on this! Drop everything else! Twelve-hour shifts! We won't stop until we've accounted for every penny they owe us!"

Agent Brown was tactful enough not to point out that there was no evidence whatsoever at this time that Agrafan and Netter had cheated Uncle Sam. Agent Smith also said nothing to his boss, but, an hour later, he phoned Goll, the butler. Smith told Goll all that had happened and was likely to happen. Goll thanked him and said that $200,000 in cash would arrive at Smith's mailbox tomorrow. Goll then phoned his employers.

"Gnatcatcher will be getting a court order to tap our phone lines," Netter said.

"How long before the taps are installed?"

"Within an hour."

Netter cut off the phone and spoke to his partner. "Some vital data is missing from our prognosticator. We have to revise our plans. Quickly."

Agrafan said, "I'm not sure that if we start Operation Trapdoor now, it'll be successful."

"There's nothing else we can do. Also, Gnatcatcher is acting irrationally. He insists on speaking to us. Not just through the phone but face to face on the screen. He won't take no for an answer. We . . ."

Agrafan answered the phone. He listened for a moment, then said, "Thank you, Goll." To Netter, he said, "Goll just got a call from Gnatcatcher himself. Gnatcatcher says that we must talk to him face to face. He has to see us, even if only through the screen."

"Why is he so adamant about visual contact?"

"Goll said that he thinks that Gnatcatcher suspects that we two don't exist. Or perhaps he suspects that someone or some group has murdered us and is posing as us. Goll calls it the Howard Hughes syndrome."

Netter sighed from a ventral tube and flapped his wings and wiggled his antennae. "Very well. Have Goll put us through to Gnatcatcher."

"No, first we pull the lever," Agrafan said. "One call to our chief representative in Wall Street, and it's done."

That having been accomplished, Agrafan made the arrangements for the video meeting. A minute later, Gnatcatcher's face, now a near-purple, though it just looked dark on the infrared screen, appeared. But, on seeing what he thought was the two (actually, he was seeing a video simulation), his jaw dropped, his eyes bugged, and the purple changed to gray. Then the screen went blank.

"A very strange and unexpected reaction," Netter said. "What could have caused him to cut us off?"

Agrafan said, "Obviously, we lack some data."

They had been watching TV ever since the first sets

had been sold. Their favorites were old movie films, and they especially liked the antics of two film comedians who had made all their pictures before TV had become a mundane reality. Agrafan and Netter saw a parallel between their own early bumblings and mistakes on Earth and those of the two comedians. Because of their empathizing, they had used the two comedians as models for the simulations. Until now, however, they had not been forced to use these. All contacts with the world outside their room had been by phone.

How were they to know that Gnatcatcher, when he was a child and still undehumanized by forty years of IRS employment, had often seen and loved the ancient tapes of two Hollywood comics?

Brown, Smith, and Jones, burdened with fifty pounds of computer printouts, had just entered Gnatcatcher's office. Though the paper contained only a small fraction of the enormousness of what *must* be a communist plot, the three carried in their heads the summary of the terrifying and mind-spinning situation.

They were pale and tottery when they came through the door. Seeing Gnatcatcher's corpselike skin and wild eyes, they became even whiter and weaker. "What's the matter, boss?" they said in unison.

"Laurel and Hardy!" Gnatcatcher screamed.

"What?" the three said, again in unison.

Gnatcatcher did not explain. He roared. "Get me the White House! And get another court order! We're invading the house!"

"The White House, sir?" Smith said faintly.

"No, you imbecile! The house of Agrafan and Netter! Have our men armed, ready to shoot at the first sign of resistance! Can you get hold of bazookas?"

Smith said, "Yes, sir," and he staggered out to transmit the orders. First, though, he phoned Goll. The butler thanked him and said that another $200,000 would be in Smith's mailbox by tomorrow.

It was left to Brown to explain the situation to Gnatcatcher. Stammering slightly, swallowing saliva that was not there, he said, "I've never heard of or encountered such a case before, sir. It's absolutely unprecedented. I talked to their lawyers just before I came in; they explained the whole amazing business. They said that Agrafan and Netter are real patriots. They've been paying far more income tax, their businesses have, I mean, than they were required to pay. They—" He stopped.

"So what?" Gnatcatcher snarled. "We gave them the proper refund, didn't we? Nobody can say we're not honest. We always refund if we find we have to!"

"Well, it's this way, sir. Since 1952, every property they own has paid twice what they should have paid!"

"How in hell could they do that? Why didn't we catch it?"

Brown said, "Uh . . . their companies have been keeping two sets of books!"

Gnatcatcher's face was speeding toward purple again.

"That's illegal! We got them now!"

"No, sir, it's not illegal to pay Uncle Sam twice what you should. The records we've seen showed one set of profits on which they paid taxes double what we should have gotten. Their other records, the ones we hadn't seen until now, showed the true profits, the smaller ones."

"I don't believe this!" Gnatcatcher screamed. Then, calming a little, "So what? They've just made a big donation to the Treasury, that's all!"

Very quietly, Brown said, "You forget what I said, sir. About the refund. They're calling in the chips. They want every cent of their overpayment. There's no time limit on it, sir, like there used to be. The good news is that they're not asking for interest earned on the overpayment, though I don't think it would do them any good to ask.''

"That's fraud, collusion, and God knows what other hideous crimes against the state!'' Gnatcatcher bellowed. "They can't get away with it! We'll take them to court! They'll get bounced so quick—no way is—'' He paused, struggled for breath, clutched his stomach, then said, "What is the total sum of this alleged overpayment?''

Brown opted out of answering by fainting. While he was being revived, agent Jones said, "Uh, the exact sum is eight hundred billion, ninety-six million, twenty-seven thousand, six hundred and three dollars and thirty cents, sir!''

It was Gnatcatcher's turn to faint. When he came to, he muttered, "Rally around the flag, boys.''

A minute later, having recovered somewhat, he said, "We've got to squash this, nip it in the bud. It's sheer nonsense, gibberish, mopery on a colossal scale. But the mere rumor that this situation existed would cause the stock market to crash. We'll keep this quiet among us, men. And we'll go out and burn the traitors' house down! That'll put a stop to it!''

"Their lawyers and whoever runs their empire for them know about this,'' Jones said.

"None of their underlings'll dare say a word about it or about a refund after I get through talking to them!'' Gnatcatcher screamed. Still holding his belly, he said, "We're going to storm their house, drag them out, doctors' excuses or no excuses, slam them into jail, incognito! I mean incommunicado! Don't argue with me!''

"Their civil rights, sir?'' Brown said.

"This is war!'' Gnatcatcher shouted. "I'll get the President to declare a state of martial law, civil rights suspended during the emergency! Once he understands the full implications of this, even he, dumb as he is, will cooperate fully!''

The phone on Gnatcatcher's desk rang. Brown punched a button, and a face appeared on the screen. "Speak of the devil," Brown muttered. He turned. "The President, sir."

It was too late. If the IRS did not pay the refund, or if it fought the case in court, every company controlled by Agrafan and Netter was to unload its stocks and declare bankruptcy. That meant that the stock market would topple with a roar far louder than it had made in 1929. The world would sink into Great Depression II. All funds for space exploration, especially those for the tremendously expensive Uranus project would be cut off. Another generation, perhaps two or three, would pass before Earth endangered the life-forms of the great green planet again.

Meanwhile, Gnatcatcher and his IRS contingent were outside the house. With them were National Guard units equipped with tanks and rocket-launchers.

Agrafan and Netter radioed their farewells, knowing that they would probably be dead before the message reached home.

"Well, it's not so bad to end this," Netter said. "I've been suffering from the heat ever since I got here. Now, I'll be comfortable. Death is comfortable, isn't it?"

"We'll find out," Agrafan said. "Anyway, there's usually something good to say about any situation. Don't the Earth people have a word for that attitude?"

"Pollyanna."

"I had a teacher named that. No connection, of course."

"Don't die thinking that," Netter said. "It makes it seem that you've learned nothing, wasted your life. All things impinge. Nothing moves without being moved or moving other things."

"Sorry," Agrafan said. "I've been here too long. I'm starting to think like *them*."

Agrafan punched a button. Its last thought was of home, of the deliciously cold clouds, of flying through them, of ecstasy felt when he had been young and foolish and had dived as deep as he could, coming dangerously close to the hot, liquid hydrogen layer. Earth people did not know what fun was.

The insulated room with its frozen carbon dioxide furniture and emergency bottles of methane-hydrogen-helium gas and the TV set with the infrared screen vanished in a gout of flame. Nothing would be left for the Earth people to identify Agrafan and Netter as nonterrestrials.

Gnatcatcher ran as fast as he could, but the heat, far greater than that in his belly, caught up with him and passed him.

The Making of
Revelation, Part I

God said, "Bring me Cecil B. DeMille."

"Dead or alive?" the angel Gabriel said.

"I want to make him an offer he can't refuse. Can even *I* do this to a dead man?"

"Oh, I see," said Gabriel, who didn't. "It will be done."

And it was.

Cecil Blount DeMille, confused, stood in front of the desk. He didn't like it. He was used to sitting behind the desk while others stood. Considering the circumstances, he wasn't about to protest. The giant, divinely handsome, bearded, pipe-smoking man behind the desk was not one you'd screw around with. However, the gray eyes, though steely, weren't quite those of a Wall Street banker. They held a hint of compassion.

Unable to meet those eyes, DeMille looked at the angel by his side. He'd always thought angels had wings. This one didn't, though he could certainly fly. He'd carried DeMille in his arms up through the stratosphere to a city of gold somewhere between the Earth and the moon. Without a space suit, too.

God, like all great entities, came right to the point.

"This is 1980 A.D. In twenty years it'll be time for The Millennium. The day of judgement. The events as depicted in the Book of Revelation or the Apocalypse by St. John the Divine. You know, the seven seals, the four horsemen, the moon dripping blood, Armageddon, and all that.''

DeMille wished he'd be invited to sit down. Being dead for twenty-one years, during which he'd not moved a muscle, had tended to weaken him.

"Take a chair," God said. "Gabe, bring the man a brandy." He puffed on his pipe; tiny lightning crackled through the clouds of smoke.

"Here you are, Mr. DeMille," Gabriel said, handing him the liqueur in a cut quartz goblet. "Napoleon 1880.''

DeMille knew there wasn't any such thing as a one-hundred-year-old brandy, but he didn't argue. Anyway, the stuff certainly tasted like it was. They really lived up here.

God sighed, and he said, "The main trouble is that not many people really believe in Me any more. So My powers are not what they once were. The old gods, Zeus, Odin, all that bunch, lost their strength and just faded away, like old soldiers, when their worshippers ceased to believe in them.

"So, I just can't handle the end of the world by Myself any more. I need someone with experience, know-how, connections, and a reputation. Somebody people know really existed. You. Unless you know of somebody who's made more Biblical epics than you have.''

"That'll be the day," DeMille said. "But what about the unions? They really gave me a hard time, the commie bas . . . uh, so-and-so's. Are they as strong as ever?''

"You wouldn't believe their clout nowadays.''

DeMille bit his lip, then said, "I want them dissolved. If I only got twenty years to produce this film, I can't be held up by a bunch of goldbrickers."

"No way," God said. "They'd all strike, and we can't afford any delays."

He looked at his big railroad watch. "We're going to be on a very tight schedule."

"Well, I don't know," DeMille said. "You can't get anything done with all their regulations, interunion jealousies, and the featherbedding. And the wages! It's no wonder it's so hard to show a profit. It's too much of a hassle!"

"I can always get D. W. Griffith."

DeMille's face turned red. "You want a grade-B production? No, no, that's all right! I'll do it, do it!"

God smiled and leaned back. "I thought so. By the way, you're not the producer, too; I am. My angels will be the executive producers. They haven't had much to do for several millennia, and the devil makes work for idle hands, you know. Haw, haw! You'll be the chief director, of course. But this is going to be quite a job. You'll have to have at least a hundred thousand assistant directors."

"But . . . that means training about 99,000 directors!"

"That's the least of our problems. Now you can see why I want to get things going immediately."

DeMille gripped the arms of the chair and said, weakly, "Who's going to finance this?"

God frowned. "That's another problem. My Antagonist has control of all the banks. If worse comes to worse, I could melt down the heavenly city and sell it. But the bottom of the gold market would drop all the way to hell. And I'd have to move to Beverly Hills. You wouldn't believe the smog there or the prices they're asking for houses.

"However, I think I can get the money. Leave that to Me."

The men who really owned the American banks sat at a long mahogany table in a huge room in a Manhattan skyscraper. The Chairman of the Board sat at the head. He didn't have the horns, tail, and hooves which legend gave him. Nor did he have an odor of brimstone. More like Brut. He was devilishly handsome and the biggest and best-built man in the room. He looked like he could have been the chief of the angels and in fact once had been. His eyes were evil but no more so than the others at the table, bar one.

The exception, Raphael, sat at the other end of the table. The only detractions from his angelic appearance were his bloodshot eyes. His apartment on the West Side had paper-thin walls, and the swingers' party next door had kept him awake most of the night. Despite his fatigue, he'd been quite effective in presenting the offer from above.

Don Francisco "The Fixer" Fica drank a sixth glass of wine to up his courage, made the sign of the cross, most offensive to the Chairman, gulped, and spoke.

"I'm sorry, Signor, but that's the way the vote went. One hundred percent. It's a purely business proposition, legal, too, and there's no way we won't make a huge profit from it. We're gonna finance the movie, come hell or high water!"

Satan reared up from his chair and slammed a huge but well-manicured fist onto the table. Glasses of vino crashed over; plates half-filled with pasta and spaghetti rattled. All but Raphael paled.

"*Dio motarello! Lecaculi! Cacasotti! Non romperci i coglioni!* I'm the Chairman, and I say no, no, no!"

Fica looked at the other heads of the families. Mig-

---

notta, Fregna, Stronza, Loffa, Recchione, and Bocchino seemed scared, but each nodded the go-ahead at Fica.

"I'm indeed sorry that you don't see it our way," Fica said. "But I must ask for your resignation."

Only Raphael could meet The Big One's eyes, but business was business. Satan cursed and threatened. Nevertheless, he was stripped of all his shares of stock. He'd walked in the richest man in the world, and he stormed out penniless and an ex-member of the Organization.

Raphael caught up with him as he strode mumbling up Park Avenue.

"You're the father of lies," Raphael said, "so you can easily be a great success as an actor or politician. There's money in both fields. Fame, too. I suggest acting. You've got more friends in Hollywood than anywhere else."

"Are you nuts?" Satan snarled.

"No. Listen. I'm authorized to sign you up for the film on the end of the world. You'll be a lead, get top billing. You'll have to share it with The Son, but we can guarantee you a bigger dressing room than His. You'll be playing yourself, so it ought to be easy work."

Satan laughed so loudly that he cleared the sidewalks for two blocks. The Empire State Building swayed more than it should have in the wind.

"You and your boss must think I'm pretty dumb! Without me the film's a flop. You're up a creek without a paddle. Why should I help you? If I do I end up at the bottom of a flaming pit forever. Bug off!"

Raphael shouted after him, "We can always get Roman Polanski!"

Raphael reported to God, who was taking His ease on His jasper and cornelian throne above which glowed a rainbow.

"He's right, Your Divinity. If he refuses to cooperate, the whole deal's off. No real Satan, no real Apocalypse."

_____

God smiled. "We'll see."

Raphael wanted to ask Him what He had in mind. But an angel appeared with a request that God come to the special effects department. Its technicians were having trouble with the roll-up-the-sky-like-a-scroll machine.

"Schmucks!" God growled. "Do I have to do everything?"

Satan moved into a tenement on 121st Street and went on welfare. It wasn't a bad life, not for one who was used to Hell. But two months later, his checks quit coming. There was no unemployment any more. Anyone who was capable of working but wouldn't was out of luck. What had happened was that Central Casting had hired everybody in the world as production workers, stars, bit players, or extras.

Meanwhile, all the advertising agencies in the world had spread the word, good or bad depending upon the viewpoint, that the Bible was true. If you weren't a Christian, and, what was worse, a sincere Christian, you were doomed to perdition.

Raphael shot up to Heaven again.

"My God, You wouldn't believe what's happening! The Christians are repenting of their sins and promising to be good forever and ever, amen! The Jews, Moslems, Hindus, Buddhists, scientologists, animists, you name them, are lining up at the baptismal fonts! What a mess! The atheists have converted, too, and all the communist and Marxian socialist governments have been overthrown!"

"That's nice," God said. "But I'll really believe in the sincerity of the Christian nations when they kick out their present administrations. Down to the local dogcatcher."

"They're doing it!" Raphael shouted. "But maybe You don't understand! This isn't the way things go in the *Book of Revelation*! We'll have to do some very extensive re-writing of the script! Unless You straighten things out!''

God seemed very calm. "The script? How's Ellison coming along with it?''

Of course, God knew everything that was happening, but He pretended sometimes that He didn't. It was His excuse for talking. Just issuing a command every once in a while made for long silences, sometimes lasting for centuries.

He had hired only science-fiction writers to work on the script since they were the only ones with imaginations big enough to handle the job. Besides, they weren't bothered by scientific impossibilities. God loved Ellison, the head writer, because he was the only human he'd met so far who wasn't afraid to argue with Him. Ellison was severely handicapped, however, because he wasn't allowed to use obscenities while in His presence.

"Ellison's going to have a hemorrhage when he finds out about the rewrites,'' Raphael said. "He gets screaming mad if anyone messes around with his scripts.''

"I'll have him up for dinner,'' God said. "If he gets too obstreperous, I'll toss around a few lightning bolts. If he thinks he was burned before . . . Well!''

Raphael wanted to question God about the tampering with the book, but just then the head of Budgets came in. The angel beat it. God got very upset when He had to deal with money matters.

The head assistant director said, "We got a big problem now, Mr. DeMille. We can't have any Armageddon. Israel's willing to rent the site to us, but where are we going to get the forces of Gog and Magog to fight against the good guys? Everybody's converted. Nobody's willing to fight on the side of anti-Christ and Satan. That means we've got to change the script again. I don't want to be the one to tell Ellison . . .''

"Do I have to think of everything?" DeMille said. "It's no problem: Just hire actors to play the villains."

"I already thought of that. But they want a bonus. They say they might be persecuted just for *playing* the guys in the black hats. They call it the social-stigma bonus. But the guilds and the unions won't go for it. Equal pay for all extras or no movie and that's that."

DeMille sighed. "It won't make any difference anyway as long as we can't get Satan to play himself."

The assistant nodded. So far, they'd been shooting around the devil's scenes. But they couldn't put it off much longer.

DeMille stood up. "I have to watch the auditions for The Great Whore of Babylon."

The field of 100,000 candidates for the role had been narrowed to a hundred, but from what he'd heard none of these could play the part. They were all good Christians now, no matter what they'd been before, and they just didn't have their hearts in the role. DeMille had intended to cast his brand-new mistress, a starlet, a hot little number—if promises meant anything—one hundred percent right for the part. But just before they went to bed for the first time, he'd gotten a phone call.

"None of this hankypanky, C.B.," God had said. "You're now a devout worshipper of Me, one of the lost sheep that's found its way back to the fold. So get with it. Otherwise, back to Forest Lawn for you, and I use Griffith."

"But . . . but I'm Cecil B. DeMille! The rules are O.K. for the common people, but . . ."

"Throw that scarlet woman out! Shape up or ship out! If you marry her, fine! But remember, there'll be no more divorces!"

DeMille was glum. Eternity was going to be like living forever next door to the Board of Censors.

The next day, his secretary, very excited, buzzed him.

"Mr. DeMille! Satan's here! I don't have him for an appointment, but he says he's always had a long-standing one with you!"

Demoniac laughter bellowed through the intercom.

"C.B., my boy! I've changed my mind! I tried out anonymously for the part, but your shithead assistant said I wasn't the type for the role! So I've come to you! I can start work as soon as we sign the contract!"

The contract, however, was not the one the great director had in mind. Satan, smoking a big cigar, chuckling, cavorting, read the terms.

"And don't worry about signing in your blood. It's unsanitary. Just ink in your John Henry, and all's well that ends in Hell."

"You get my soul," DeMille said weakly.

"It's not much of a bargain for me. But if you don't sign it, you won't get me. Without me, the movie's a bomb. Ask The Producer, He'll tell you how it is."

"I'll call Him now."

"No! Sign now, this very second, or I walk out forever!"

DeMille bowed his head, more in pain than in prayer.

"Now!"

DeMille wrote on the dotted line. There had never been any genuine indecision. After all, he was a film director.

After snickering Satan had left, DeMille punched a phone number. The circuits transmitted this to a station which beamed the pulses up to a satellite which transmitted these directly to the heavenly city. Somehow, he got a wrong number. He hung up quickly when Israfel, the angel of death, answered. The second attempt, he got through.

"Your Divinity, I suppose. You know what I just did? It *was* the only way you could get him to play himself. You understand that, don't You?"

"Yes, but if you're thinking of breaking the contract or getting Me to do it for you, forget it. What kind of an image would I have if I did something unethical like that? But not to worry. He can't get his hooks into your soul until I say so."

Not to worry? DeMille thought. I'm the one who's going to Hell, not Him.

"Speaking of hooks, let Me remind you of a clause in your contract with The Studio. If you ever fall from grace, and I'm not talking about that little bimbo you were going to make your mistress, you'll die. The Mafia isn't the only one that puts out a contract. *Capice?*"

DeMille, sweating and cold, hung up. In a sense, he was already in Hell. All his life with no women except for one wife? It was bad enough to have no variety, but what if whoever he married cut him off, like one of his wives—what was her name?—had done?

Moreover, he couldn't get loaded out of his skull even to forget his marital woes. God, though not prohibiting booze in His Book, had said that moderation in strong liquor was required and no excuses. Well, maybe he could drink beer, however disgustingly plebeian that was.

He wasn't even happy with his work now. He just didn't get the respect he had in the old days. When he chewed out the camerapeople, the grips, the gaffers, the actors, they stormed back at him that he didn't have the proper Christian humility, he was too high and mighty, too arrogant. God would get him if he didn't watch his big fucking mouth.

This left him speechless and quivering. He'd always thought, and acted accordingly, that the director, not God, was God. He remembered telling Charlton Heston that when Heston, who after all was only Moses, had thrown a temper tantrum when he'd stepped in a pile of camel shit during the filming of *The Ten Commandments*.

Was there more to the making of the end-of-the-world than appeared on the surface? Had God seemingly forgiven everybody their sins and lack of faith but was subtly, even insidiously, making everybody pay by suffering? Had He forgiven but not forgotten? Or vice versa?

God marked even the fall of a sparrow, though why the sparrow, a notoriously obnoxious and dirty bird, should be significant in God's eye was beyond DeMille.

He had the uneasy feeling that everything wasn't as simple and as obvious as he'd thought when he'd been untimely ripped from the grave in a sort of Caesarean section and carried off like a nursing baby in Gabriel's arms to the office of The Ultimate Producer

From the *Playboy* Interview feature, December, 1980.

Playboy: Mr. Satan, why did you decide to play yourself after all?

Satan: Damned if I know.

Playboy: The rumors are that you'll be required to wear clothes in the latter-day scenes but that you steadfastly refuse. Are these rumors true?

Satan: Yes indeed. Everybody knows I never wear clothes except when I want to appear among humans without attracting undue attention. If I wear clothes it'd be unrealistic. It'd be phoney, though God knows there are enough fake things in this movie. The Producer says this is going to be a PG picture, not an X-rated. That's why I walked off the set the other day. My lawyers are negotiating with The Studio now about this. But you can bet your ass that I won't go back unless things go my way, the right way. After all, I am an artist, and I have my integrity. Tell me, if you had a prong this size, would you hide it?

Playboy: The Chicago cops would arrest me before I got a block from my pad. I don't know, though,

if they'd charge me with indecent exposure or being careless with a natural resource.

Satan: They wouldn't dare arrest me. I got too much
on the city administration.

Playboy: That's some whopper. But I thought angels
were sexless. You are a fallen angel, aren't you?

Satan: You jerk! What kind of researcher are you?
Right there in the Bible, *Genesis* 6:2, it says that
the sons of God, that is, the angels, took the
daughters of men as wives and had children by
them. You think the kids were test tube babies?
Also, you dunce, I refer you to *Jude 7* where it's
said that the angels, like the Sodomites, committed
fornications and followed unnatural lusts.

Playboy: Whew! That brimstone! There's no need getting so hot under the collar, Mr. Satan. I only converted a few years ago. I haven't had much chance
to read the Bible.

Satan: I read the Bible every day. All of it. I'm a
speedreader, you know.

Playboy: You read the Bible? (Pause.) Hee, hee! Do
you read it for the same reason W. C. Fields did
when he was dying?

Satan: What's that?

Playboy: Looking for loopholes.

DeMille was in a satellite and supervising the camerapeople while they shot the takes from ten miles up. He
didn't like at all the terrific pressure he was working
under. There was no chance to shoot every scene three
or four times to get the best angle. Or to reshoot if the
actors blew their lines. And, oh, sweet Jesus, they were
blowing them all over the world!

He mopped his bald head. "I don't care what The
Producer says! We have to retake at least a thousand
scenes. And we've a million miles of film to go yet!"

They were getting close to the end of the breaking-of-the-seven-seals sequences. The Lamb, played by The Producer's Son, had just broken the sixth seal. The violent worldwide earthquake had gone well. The sun-turning-black-as-a-funeral-pall had been a breeze. But the moon-all-red-as-blood had had some color problems. The rushes looked more like Colonel Sanders' orange juice than hemoglobin. In DeMille's opinion the stars-falling-to-earth-like-figs-shaken-down-by-a-gale scenes had been excellent, visually speaking. But everybody knew that the stars were not little blazing stones set in the sky but were colossal balls of atomic fires each of which was many times bigger than Earth. Even one of them, a million miles from Earth, would destroy it. So where was the credibility factor?

"I don't understand you, boss," DeMille's assistant said. "You didn't worry about credibility when you made *The Ten Commandments*. When Heston, I mean, Moses, parted the Red Sea, it was the fakiest thing I ever saw. It must've made unbelievers out of millions of Christians. But the film was a box-office success."

"It was the dancing girls that brought off the whole thing!" DeMille screamed. "Who cares about all that other bullshit when they can see all those beautiful long-legged snatches twirling their veils!"

His secretary floated from her chair. "I quit, you male chauvinistic pig! So me and my sisters are just snatches to you, you baldheaded cunt?"

His hotline to the heavenly city rang. He picked up the phone.

"Watch your language!" The Producer thundered. "If you step out of line too many times, I'll send you back to the grave! And Satan gets you right then and there!"

Chastened but boiling near the danger point, DeMille got back to business, called Art in Hollywood. The sweep of the satellite around Earth included the sky-vanishing-

as-a-scroll-is-rolled-up scenes, where every-mountain-
and-island-is-removed-from-its-place. If the script had
called for a literal removing, the tectonics problem would
have been terrific and perhaps impossible. But in this
case the special effects departments only had to simulate
the scenes.

Even so, the budget was strained. However, The Producer, through his unique abilities, was able to carry
these off. Whereas, in the original script, genuine dis-
placements of Greenland, England, Ireland, Japan, and
Madagascar had been called for, not to mention thousands of smaller islands, these were only faked.

"Your Divinity, I have some bad news," Raphael said.

The Producer was too busy to indulge in talking about
something He already knew. Millions of the faithful had
backslid and taken up their old sinful ways. They believed that since so many events of the Apocalypse were
being faked, God must not be capable of making any
really big catastrophes. So, they didn't have anything to
worry about.

The Producer, however, had decided that it would not
only be good to wipe out some of the wicked but it would
strengthen the faithful if they saw that God still had some
muscle.

"They'll get the real thing next time," He said. "But
we have to give DeMille time to set up his cameras at
the right places. And we'll have to have the script rewritten, of course."

Raphael groaned. "Couldn't somebody else tell Ellison? He'll carry on something awful."

"I'll tell him. You look pretty pooped, Rafe. You need
a little R&R. Take two weeks off. But don't do it on
Earth. Things are going to be very unsettling there for a
while."

Raphael, who had a tender heart, said, "Thanks, Boss. I'd just as soon not be around to see it."

The seal was stamped on the foreheads of the faithful, marking them safe from the burning of a third of Earth, the turning of a third of the sea to blood along with the sinking of a third of the ships at sea (which also included the crashing of a third of the airplanes in the air, something St. John had overlooked), the turning of a third of all water to wormwood (a superfluous measure since a third was already thoroughly polluted), the failure of a third of daylight, the release of giant mutant locusts from the abyss, and the release of poison-gas-breathing mutant horses, which slew a third of mankind.

DeMille was delighted. Never had such terrifying scenes been filmed. And these were nothing to the plagues which followed. He had enough film from the cutting room to make a hundred documentaries after the movie was shown. And then he got a call from The Producer.

"It's back to the special effects, my boy."

"But why, Your Divinity? We still have to shoot The-Great-Whore-of-Babylon sequences, the two-Beasts-and-the-marking-of-the-wicked, the Mount-Zion-and-The-Lamb-with-His-one-hundred-and-forty-thousand-good-men-who-haven't-defiled-themselves-with-women, the . . ."

"Because there aren't any wicked left by now, you dolt! And not too many of the good, either!"

"That couldn't be helped," DeMille said. "Those gas-breathing, scorpion-tailed horses kind of got out of hand. But we just *have* to have the scenes where the rest of mankind that survives the plagues still doesn't abjure its worship of idols and doesn't repent of its murders, sorcery, fornications, and robberies."

"Rewrite the script."

"Ellison will quit for sure this time."

"That's all right. I already have some hack from Peoria lined up to take his place. And cheaper, too."

DeMille took his outfit, one hundred thousand strong, to the heavenly city. Here they shot the war between Satan and his demons and Michael and his angels. This was not in the chronological sequence as written by St. John. But the logistics problems were so tremendous that it was thought best to film these out of order.

Per the rewritten script, Satan and his host were defeated, but a lot of nonbelligerents were casualities, including DeMille's best cameraperson. Moreover, there was a delay in production when Satan insisted that a stuntperson do the part where he was hurled from Heaven to Earth.

"Or use a dummy!" he yelled. "Twenty thousand miles is a hell of a long way to fall! If I'm hurt badly I might not be able to finish the movie!"

The screaming match between the director and Satan took place on the edge of the city. The Producer, unnoticed, came up behind Satan and kicked him from the city for the second time in their relationship with utter ruin and furious combustion.

Shrieking, "I'll sue! I'll sue!" Satan fell towards the planet below. He made a fine spectacle in his blazing entrance into the atmosphere, but the people on Earth paid it little attention. They were used to fiery portents in the sky. In fact, they were getting fed up with them.

DeMille screamed and danced around and jumped up and down. Only the presence of The Producer kept him from using foul and abusive language.

"We didn't get it on camera! Now we'll have to shoot it over!"

"His contract calls for only one fall," God said. "You'd better shoot the War-between-The-Faithful-and-True-Rider-against-the-beast-and-the-false-prophet while he recovers."

"What'll I do about the fall?" DeMille moaned.

"Fake it," The Producer said, and He went back to His office.

Per the script, an angel came down from Heaven and bound up the badly injured and burned and groaning Satan with a chain and threw him into the abyss, the Grand Canyon. Then he shut and sealed it over him (what a terrific sequence that was!) so that Satan might seduce the nations no more until a thousand years had passed.

A few years later the devil's writhings caused a volcano to form above him, and the Environmental Protection Agency filed suit against Celestial Productions, Inc. because of the resultant pollution of the atmosphere.

Then God, very powerful now that only believers existed on Earth, performed the first resurrection. In this, only the martyrs were raised. And Earth, which had had much elbow room because of the recent wars and plagues, was suddenly crowded again.

Part I was finished except for the reshooting of some scenes, the dubbing in of voice and background noise, and the synchronization of the music, which was done by the cherubim and seraphim (all now unionized).

The great night of the premiere in a newly built theater in Hollywood, six million capacity, arrived. DeMille got a standing ovation after it was over. But *Time* and *Newsweek* and *The Manchester Guardian* panned the movie.

"There are some people who may go to Hell after all," God growled.

DeMille didn't care about that. The film was a box-office success, grossing ten billion dollars in the first six months. And when he considered the reruns in theaters and the TV rights . . . well, had anyone ever done better?

He had a thousand more years to live. That seemed

like a long time. Now. But . . . what would happen to him when Satan was released to seduce the nations again? According to John the Divine's book, there'd be another worldwide battle. Then Satan, defeated, would be cast into the lake of fire and sulphur in the abyss.

(He'd be allowed to keep his Oscar, however.)

Would God let Satan, per the contract DeMille had signed with the devil, take DeMille with him into the abyss? Or would He keep him safe long enough to finish directing Part II? After Satan was buried for good, there'd be a second resurrection and a judging of those raised from the dead. The goats, the bad guys, would be hurled into the pit to keep Satan company. DeMille should be with the saved, the sheep, because he had been born again. But there was that contract with The Tempter.

DeMille arranged a conference with The Producer. Ostensibly, it was about Part II, but DeMille managed to bring up the subject which really interested him.

"I can't break your contract with him," God said.

"But I only signed it so that You'd be sure to get Satan for the role. It was a self-sacrifice. Greater love hath no man and all that. Doesn't that count for anything?"

"Let's discuss the shooting of the new Heaven and the new Earth sequences."

At least I'm not going to be put into Hell until the movie is done, DeMille thought. But after that? He couldn't endure thinking about it.

"It's going to be a terrible technical problem," God said, interrupting DeMille's gloomy thoughts. "When the second resurrection takes place, there won't be even Standing Room Only on Earth. That's why I'm dissolving the old Earth and making a new one. But I can't just duplicate the old Earth. The problem of Lebensraum would still remain. Now, what I'm contemplating is a Dyson sphere."

"What's that?"

"A scheme by a 20th-century mathematician to break up the giant planet Jupiter into large pieces and set them in orbit at the distance of Earth from the sun. The surfaces of the pieces would provide room for a population enormously larger than Earth's. It's a Godlike concept."

"What a documentary its filming would be!" DeMille said. "Of course, if we could write some love interest in it, we could make a he . . . pardon me, a heaven of a good story!"

God looked at his big railroad watch.

"I have another appointment, C.B. The conference is over."

DeMille said good-bye and walked dejectedly towards the door. He still hadn't gotten an answer about his ultimate fate. God was stringing him along. He felt that he wouldn't know until the last minute what was going to happen to him. He'd be suffering a thousand years of uncertainty, of mental torture. His life would be a cliffhanger. Will God relent? Or will He save the hero at the very last second?

"C.B.," God said.

DeMille spun around, his heart thudding, his knees turned to water. Was this it? The fatal finale? Had God, in His mysterious and subtle way, decided for some reason that there'd be no Continued In Next Chapter for him? It didn't seem likely, but then The Producer had never promised that He'd use him as the director of Part II nor had He signed a contract with him. Maybe, like so many temperamental producers, He'd suddenly concluded that DeMille wasn't the right one for the job. Which meant that He could arrange it so that his ex-director would be thrown now, right this minute, into the lake of fire.

God said, "I can't break your contract with Satan. So . . . "

"Yes?"

DeMille's voice sounded to him as if he were speaking very far away.

"Satan can't have your soul until you die."

"Yes?"

His voice was only a trickle of sound, a last few drops of water from a clogged drainpipe.

"So, if you don't die, and that, of course, depends upon your behavior, Satan can't ever have your soul."

God smiled and said, "See you in eternity."

The Long Wet
Purple Dream of
Rip Van Winkle

Washington Irving did not know it. Rip did not dare tell it.

Rip hadn't been asleep every day of those twenty years. At least, he didn't think he had. Sometimes he wondered if the reality had just been pleasant, indeed, ecstatic, dreams mixed with nightmares.

In A.D. 1772, Rip was thirty-five when he passed out from the booze snitched from the strange little men playing ninepins. When he awoke on the Kaatskill meadow, his whiskers were no longer than if a night had passed. The bowlers and his dog Wolf were gone. Wincing at every step because of his hangover, he reluctantly trudged over the hills, his hunting musket on his shoulder, headed for the Hudson River and home. And the hell his wife would give him.

Suddenly, he reeled, and he cried out. The world had become all flux and also fogged with a very pale purple haze which did not obscure other colors. The leaves of the trees changed from green to many colors. Autumn fell like a dead bird and then snow dived after it. He was up to his waist in it, but he couldn't feel it. The snow melted. And snow fell again and again. The rains came; the land greened. The sun, the moon, and the stars raced across the sky.

Once a falling tree hurtled *through* him. Then it decayed and was gone while he yelled with terror and for mercy. He'd been bewitched by the little bowlers and justly so. He should've stayed home, repaired the fences and house, tilled and planted instead of lazing around, hunting, and thinking of forbidden cunt.

Suddenly, the purple haze was gone. The moon slowed and soon resumed its normal pace. All was stable again. The hot summer night was noisy with insects and a great humming from the east. Trembling, he resumed his trip home. Presently, he stopped on a hill which looked down on the river, sparkling in the full moon. The narrow dirt road along the Hudson was now a broad highway of some kind of stone. It was brightly illuminated by lights at the tops of poles along it and by lamps in the fronts of . . . *horseless carriages*? The humming was the sound they made when heard from a distance, and they were going incredibly fast.

To his right, on top of an empty hill he'd passed yesterday, was a big house with many lights and people on the front porch and a very strange music emanating from it.

Rip went down the hill slowly and quietly. He was determined to get, somehow, through all these frightening witcheries to his village, where the holy presence of the church building would make them all disappear. But he stopped at the foot of the hill. Parked in a grove of trees was one of those scary vehicles, a topless one. Its lights were out. He crept forward until he saw by the moon that a woman was sitting in the back seat. She was smoking tobacco in a little white tube. He could hear an unfamiliar but stirring music, then someone shouting, "Hiyo, Silver! Away!"

Closer, he found that the sounds came from a box in the front part of the carriage.

He looked down past the woman's right shoulder. Her skirt was up over her waist, and her hand was working up and down slowly inside some very thin lacy garments covering her loins. Her thighs gleamed whitely between the tops of her stockings—silk!—and the lacy garment. Her head was thrown back, the glowing tube sticking straight up, and she was moaning.

Rip was very embarrassed, but his tallywhacker was rising. Dame van Winkle had cut him off after the birth of their eighth; it'd been a long time since he'd gone to bed with her. Or anyone.

Rip turned to retreat, and his musket stock banged against the metal door. The woman screamed. He started to run away, but his ankle turned, and he fell flat on his face. The next he knew, something cold and hard was pressed against his neck. He looked up at the woman. She was very pretty, big-busted, and enticing in that short shameless tight dress. The huge strange-looking pistol she held was not so alluring.

She spat out invective with a vigor matched only by Mrs. van Winkle, who, however, would never have used such dirty words or blasphemous oaths. Then she let him get to his feet.

Eyes wide, she said, "What kind of crazy outfit is that? Are you a butler from that house?" Then, seeing the musket, she cried, "What in hell is that?"

He tried to explain. When she'd heard him out, she said, "Your name is *Rip van Winkle*? Now I know you're a refugee from the funny farm."

"There's no farmer around here by that name," he said, "unless you mean Klaus van Fannij."

She looked at the tiny watch on her wrist. "Shit! Isn't

he ever coming back? I get so goddam fed up waiting around for him while he's sneaking around spying on those big-shot crooks!''

She backed up to the car, reached behind to the rear seat, and brought up a silver flask. She unscrewed the cap of the flask with a thumb, and, still pointing the enormous weapon at him, drank deeply. He smelled gin.

''Here. Have a snort.''

He took it gratefully. It *was* gin but terrible stuff. Still, it helped get rid of the shakes, and it warmed the cockles of his heart, not to mention those of his tallywhacker. She saw the expanding bulge; the barrel of her gun dropped as his barrel ascended.

She took the flask back, drained it, then looked at her timepiece again. ''Well, why not? It'll serve him right,'' she said, her words slightly blurred. ''Okay. Knee-britches. Off with them.''

''My God!'' she said as they climbed into the back seat. ''It must be at least fourteen inches long!''

''Why, that's only normal,'' he said. ''You should see Brom Dutcher's!''

She laughed and said, ''Did you fall asleep and wake up in the twentieth century, Rip?''

He didn't know what she was talking about and didn't care much. After the second time, she offered him a tube which she called a Lucky Strike. He smoked it, but the paper came off on his lip and the tobacco tasted vile.

''I suppose,'' she said, ''you think I'm promiscuous. You know, fucking a complete stranger.''

He blushed. Such language from a woman!

''That loony son of a bitch runs around at night in his black hat and cloak, cackling, sneaking around, just itching to blast crooks with his two big .45 automatics. He's knocked off a lot of them, you know.'' (Rip didn't know.) ''I suppose he does much good, socially speaking. But he sure doesn't do me any good. Won't give me a tumble though I practically rub his nose in it. He's not a fairy, so I figure he's either asexual or he thinks his profession, rubbing out gangsters, is holy, just like a priest's, and he's vowed to chastity, too.

"Cranston uses me to spy for him, but he won't let me go with him when he expects some real action. He says it's not women's work, the asshole!"

"Don't he know you're doing this behind his back?" Rip said as he started plugging again.

"He should. He claims to be the only one in the world who knows what evil lurks in the hearts of men. And of women, too. Oh, wow! Oh, God! Pour it in, Knee-britches!"

Maniacal laughter, shuddery and sinister, burst from the shadows. Rip sprang up, dived over the door, jetting, landed on the ground, got up, and began to pull his britches on. The woman, muttering curses, sat up and smoothed her skirt down. A tall man, lean, hawk-faced, with a huge curving nose and wild burning eyes, appeared out of the darkness. He was dressed in strange clothes and carried a bundle under one arm. Rip supposed that was the hat and cloak the woman had mentioned.

"Margo, what do we have here?" the man said. Suddenly, a gun like the woman's was in his long pale hand.

"Some nut who claims to be Rip van Winkle, Lamont."

"I've stirred up a hornet's nest back there. They'll be on our necks in a minute. Let's go!"

Rip said, "Could you drop me off at my village? It's just down the road a mile or so."

The man waved the gun. "Get in the car. You're going to the city with us. I think you're a part of the plot, though I'll admit I don't exactly know how you fit in."

"Oh, Lamont!" the woman said. "Don't be so fucking paranoid! He's been to a masquerade party or he escaped from the puzzle factory or he *is* a time traveler!''

''You've been reading too much of that trashy science fiction. No. He's going with us. I'm getting to the bottom of this if it kills him.''

Rip prayed as he held on to the side of the door and Margo's thigh. He was traveling at a speed the philosophers had said no human being could endure. The air rushing over the glass shield in front of him smote him. The lights of the oncoming traffic were blinding.

The nightmare voyage got worse every second. Then they were crossing a gigantic steel bridge over the Hudson. Manhattan was before him, but the island, which had been nothing but woods here, was packed with incredibly high buildings and more people in a mile's stretch than he'd seen in all his life before.

And then the purple flickering started again, the sun, moon, stars whirling, snowfall followed by rain by hot sunlight, flicker, flicker, flicker. When it stopped, he was sitting on the same street in bright day, his ass hurting where he'd fallen through the car, metal squealing, horns blasting, cursings, and the front of a car just touching his back. He had a vague impression he'd been there for a long time while countless hordes of cars had passed through his body. But these were solid, and if he didn't get to the sidewalk fast, he was going to be run over or badly beaten by the red-faced driver waving a fist at him.

When he got to the walk, he looked around. Some of the buildings he'd seen from the crazy man's car were gone, replaced by others even taller. At that moment a car pulled up to the curb near him. It was rusty and dirty with PEACE and LOVE in big letters painted on it. What Margo had called a ''radio'' during the mad journey to the city was blasting out some wild barbaric rhythms.

A young woman with a mass of frizzy yellow hair stuck her head out of its window. ''Hey, man! Far out!''

The driver was a long-haired, bushy-bearded youth wearing fringed buckskin clothes and a leather head-band. He looked like a frontiersman, an Indian fighter. The female and male in the back seat wore some kind of robes with many bright symbols woven on them. One wore on the chest a round metal object sporting the slogan: *McGovern in '72*. The slogan on the chest ornament of the other was: MAKE LOVE NOT WAR.

The driver said, "Hey man, I dig those crazy threads. You going to the demonstration?"

Rip thought he might as well say he was. He needed some friendly people to guide him in his stay in this age. Oh, Lord, propelled two hundred years into the future without a return ticket!

Rip got into the front beside the girl, who introduced herself as Judy Gardenier. She asked him if he was going as the "Spirit of 1776." He said he didn't know what she was talking about. As the car headed east on a street that hadn't existed in his time, the three passed a burning tube around. It wasn't white like Margo's Lucky Strike but brown. Its smoke had a heavy acrid odor. Judy asked him if he'd like to try the joint, and he said, "Why not?" Watching him, she said, "Man, you from the sticks? You gotta draw it way down into your lungs and hold it as long as you can."

He did so, and after a few times he began to relax. Things didn't seem so bad now.

"You got any bread?" Judy said.

"Not a bite," Rip said, and the others howled with laughter. When he found out what she meant, he produced from his pocket his worldly wealth, two copper halfpence coins. Judy looked at the King George III heads and the dates, and said, "Wow, collector's items!"

Rip let Judy keep the coins. What the hell.

The trip toward the "pad" in "Hell's Kitchen" was fascinating if sometimes shocking and always confusing.

He was startled when he saw the first black and white couple walking along, the man feeling up the woman's ass. The attitude toward slaves certainly had changed. Or did the colonists now have white slaves, too? Whatever the situation was, the color barrier was down.

Women's skirts were, however, up, way up. After he got over his first shock at seeing so much leg, he reveled in it. Nobody else seemed to think such exposure was sinful, so why should he?

The "pad" was in a basement occupied by ten or twelve youths of two or three sexes. A very short stout man with a long red beard, Yosemite Sam, seemed to be the leader.

A girl whose thin blouse obviously had nothing under it, said, "You gotta be putting me on! Rip van Winkle!"

"It's a fake name, of course," Judy said. "Rip, if you're on the run from the pigs, you're safe here. Unless there's a raid."

The four-room apartment was in bad shape, paint peeling, plaster falling, holes in the ceilings, and the furniture looked as if it had been second-hand before Noah's flood.

Everybody seemed to be having a good time, though there were some fierce cries about giving it to the fascist motherfuckers. He puffed a joint being passed around, and then an emaciated girl with huge glazed eyes asked him if he wanted some coke to snort. He said, "Yes," but when she gave him a slip of paper containing some white stuff, he sneezed, and the powder blew all over the girl. She yelled, "That'll be twenty dollars, Sneezy! The only thing I give away is my ass!"

Judy called the girl a freaking ripoff, and the next he knew Judy had thrown her out bodily. While this was going on, Rip told Yosemite Sam that he had to make water. Sam sent him to the place of convenience. But in which bowl was he supposed to urinate? The one on the floor was leaking from the base and had a big turd floating on it. Maybe it was reserved for crap only.

He retraced his steps to Sam and got him aside.

"You mean where you come from you don't have indoor plumbing? I'll bet you don't even have television!"

Rip confessed he'd never heard of either.

Mr. Sam bellowed, "Hey, everybody! Here's a dude so underprivileged you won't believe it! Gather around, folks, and hear him tell it like it is!"

Rip was very embarrassed. Besides, his bladder was hurting. "I'll be back," he muttered, and he tore loose from Sam's grip and pushed his way through to the bathroom. Still lacking instructions, he used the bowl with the pipes, one marked H, the other C. When he turned the handles, both gave cold water.

On the way back to the front room, he came to a stack of wooden crates holding books. Most had paper covers, something unfamiliar to him. The titles were strange: *The Story of O, Red Power, The World of Drugs, I Was a Black Panther for the FBI, The Mother Earth Catalog, The Annotated Fart, Lord of the Rings, Zen Archery, Love and Orgasm.*

A couple near him was arguing about UFOs, and he left the bookcase to get near enough to hear them clearly. But Judy Gardenier pulled him back to the cases, removed a volume, and showed it to him. *The Sketch Book of Geoffrey Crayon, Gent.* by Washington Irving. She opened it to a story titled—amazing—"Rip Van Winkle."

"Here. Read about your namesake."

He sat down, his back against the wall, and he slowly lip-read through the tale.

When he was done, he gazed at the wall. He couldn't believe it, but it had to be true. Irving hadn't said anything about his time-traveling. Apparently, he knew nothing about it. Irving said that he'd slept for twenty years and woke up as an old long-bearded man.

Something that especially disturbed him was that his daughter Judith had married a man named Gardenier.

Judy staggered down the hall and sat down by him.

"Kinda makes you freak out, don't it?"

"You mean that you might be my I-don't-know-how-many-times-great-granddaughter?"

"You really like to put a person on, don't you? Nah. I mean the coincidence, the names. Me Judy Gardenier and you Rip van Winkle. He *was* a fictional character, wasn't he? Even if he was real, you couldn't be him. Could you?"

"Just now I don't know who I am."

"That's right. Be cool, baby. The fuzz really after you? No matter, never mind, as Mary Baker Eddy said. Meanwhile, we're all looking for an identity."

She wanted to take him back to the front room where he could tell how he'd been disadvantaged, downtrodden, oppressed, and persecuted. Rip agreed that he'd been all that. But he didn't tell her that it wasn't the capitalist-pig class that'd been doing it to him. It was his wife. And he really couldn't blame her for hen-pecking him. He *had* been a lazy shiftless good-for-nothing who only wanted to hunt and to lounge around in front of van Vedder's tavern.

He said, "Judy, I have to ease myself again. This beer . . . what's in it? . . . I used to be able to drink a gallon before I had to go behind a tree."

He went into the bathroom and pissed in the bowl with the two pipes, idly observing that four more turds had been added to the leaking bowl. He was wondering when the honey-dipper man would come to carry the crap away when the door opened and a woman came in.

He started to protest. She screamed and ran out of the room. A minute later, two men burst in as if they expected to find a wild Indian there. They looked at Rip and started laughing. Before he could make himself decent, they seized him and carried him down the hall to the front room.

"Hey, everybody, look at this!" one of the men shouted. "This is the club Annie thought he was going to hit her with!"

The two let Rip down, and he stuffed his pisseroo into his britches and buttoned his fly. He was both embarrassed and flattered by the raucous remarks of the crowd.

The party went on and on, far past midnight. Rip wasn't used to staying awake much after dusk, but excitement kept him going. Finally, after almost everybody else had left the pad or passed out, Rip found a place behind a sofa and hurtled into sleep.

Since he was as drunk as Davy's sow, his cock should have been snakeshit-limp. He awoke, however, with his maiden's delight as hard as a tax-collector's heart, rising heaven-ward like the Tower of Babel, expanding like the British Empire. In the dim light he saw Judy, naked, crouching by him, his whacker in her hand. She certainly wasn't bobbing for apples.

Rip had always thought that this sinful act would disgust him, but it didn't. Far from it.

Judy stopped it, looked at the pulsing monolith in her hand, shrieked, and then crawled on top of him. His bumper slid into her greasy cunny as easily as a money-bag into a politician's pocket. She clamped her bunny muscle around his flailer, and they were off on the roller coaster, boxing the long compass, Eve riding Adam's tail. They came together, yelling as if the room was on fire.

After breakfast, Judy said, "The demonstration is this afternoon. This morning I'll start proceedings to get you on welfare."

She had to explain this. He was amazed. "You mean I get paid for not working?"

Judy, hearing this, laughed and said, "Rip, you're a natural-born hippie."

But his visions of paradise vanished when Judy found that he had no social security card, no ID of any kind.

"I don't know," Judy said. "Those clothes, the 1772 coins, your ignorance . . . you couldn't *really* be Rip van Winkle, could you?"

"Would you believe me if I said I was?"

"Not unless I was on something. Never mind. I'll get you a card, and you can apply. Meanwhile, how about taking a shower with me? I sold your halfpence this morning and bought some pot with part of the bread, but I used the rest of it to pay a plumber to fix up the toilet and shower."

Rip was agreeable since it seemed to him that there was more involved than just washing dirt off. He was right. This age was heaven, even if it was flawed. But then he was no perfectionist.

That afternoon he boarded a rusty old bus with about fifty others. It broke down a mile from where the parade started, and they walked the rest of the way. Rip carried a placard: DICK US NO DICKS. Judy carried: NO MORE BLOODSHED IN VIETNAM. He didn't know what the signs meant and didn't want to be ridiculed if he showed his ignorance. But it was all exciting. More had happened to him in one day than in all his life in his sleepy little village.

While he was marching along, the band playing, and he was shouting the slogans he heard the others cry out and giving the V sign, which he supposed meant, "Up yours," a beautiful redhead with huge conical tits grabbed his crotch.

"How're they, Pops? They say you're tops. You got a dong like King Kong; more jism than bishops have chrism."

Rip grinned. He felt as happy as a favorite nephew

whose rich uncle had just died, as ecstatic as a stutterer who's just had a good vowel movement. So he usually didn't know what people were talking about or what was going on most of the time? Most of the people he'd met didn't know either, since they were stoned most of the time. And so the food and liquor tasted like someone had farted in them? He could acquire a taste for them.

Suddenly, there was a lot of yelling and screaming, whistles blowing, and he was running for no reason except that everybody else was, and he was laughing like a woodpecker that'd hammered its brains out drilling for bugs in a streetlamp post. Maybe he might get his head busted or get thrown into gaol, but it was worth it. Such fun!

He threw his placard down just before summer fell away like a politician's virtue at the first bribe offered. The light purple haze swirled. Snow he couldn't feel sifted through him. Nights and days blinked like a whore batting her eyes at him. The seasons whirled around like a brindled dog chasing its tail.

"Oh, no! Not again!"

As suddenly as it had started, the gallop of time ceased. He was on the same spot and in the blaze of summer. People elbowed and jostled and groped him, but they were not those he'd left in the 70's. However, something unusual was going on. A parade of some sort. Here came a band, followed by a float bearing a huge animal figure, a funny-looking elephant, and then a group of fat elderly men dressed like Algerian pirates. Fezes, baggy pants, fake scimitars. Their leader carried a sign:

SHRINERS FOR LEX N. ORDO
AGAINST ANTI-LIFE MURDERERS

At the rear was a man dressed like the Sultan of Turkey. His sign said:

Philip José Farmer

ONE FAMILY, ONE HEAD, ONE VOTE

Behind him came marching women in white semi-military uniforms and veils. Many carried infants in their arms or jerked along toddlers. Their leader's sign said:

CHURCH, CHOW, CHILDREN

A very pregnant young woman, wearing gloves despite the heat, bumped against Rip. She snarled at him; he backed away. He glimpsed the butt of a handgun in her open handbag.

Aimlessly, he made his way through the spectators thronged along the street. It seemed to him that he'd never seen so many knocked-up women in one place. All were gloved. Was there a new custom that pregnant females had to cover their hands when in public?

He approached a very young woman, big like so many nowadays, a head taller than he. Her size wasn't her only elephantine feature. Her belly looked like she'd been carrying the baby for eighteen months.

He mumbled, "I been kind of out of things for some time. What year is this?"

She stared at him, then laughed.

"You a wino? Or you been in the slammer? It's 1987, shithead. It's also the year of the greatest infamy in history! The blackest, the lowest, the most degrading, the Naziest! That self-righteous puritanical motherfucking male-pig-chauvinist tight-assed fascist Ordo!"

"What? Who?" Rip said, trying to back away but stopped by the crowd.

"You must of been in solitary confinement! Or are you an acidhead? The President, you twit-brained prickface! That's who! He finally got the anti-abortion amendment passed! So . . . look at me! You can't even find a back-room butcher nowadays! They're scared they'll be sent up for life, and . . .''

"Here he comes!" someone shouted, and the cheering and clapping drowned out whatever else she was saying. The people were jumping up and down like barefooted sinners in hell and weeping tears bigger than horse apples. Nearby, a man, mouth frothing, eyes rolling, was down on the pavement trying to bite chunks out of the curbing. If no one else loved him, his dentist did.

First came six cars crowded with grim-faced men carrying rifles. Then a bunch of motorcycle cops. Then some armed toughs running ahead of a topless car. In its front seat were a driver and two men with set faces but nervous eyes and, in the back, a good-looking but aged woman and a man standing up and waving and grinning like an opium-smoker who'd just had a successful session in a comfort station.

The roar of the crowd pressed in on Rip like a bill-collector who's finally cornered his victim. It wasn't so loud, though, that it covered the almost simultaneous explosions of fifty—a hundred?—handguns. The big woman's pistol went off an inch from Rip's ear, causing him to crap in his pants. A second later, the gun flew high over him and landed in the street.

Rip whirled. Though deafened, he could read the woman's lips.

"There! Let the shitheads try to figure out who shot the asshole!"

Was it a conspiracy? Could a hundred women, or men, for that matter, keep a plot like that to themselves? Hell, no. A hundred pregnant women had just happened to come here with the same idea. Who knew how many more were further down the street, waiting for the chance they'd never get?

Now the guns were flying everywhere, like steel semen from a jacked-off robot. Their owners were getting rid of them and shucking their gloves, too. Their target was lying in the street, pumping blood from at least fifty holes. If he'd been an oil field, America could have told OPEC to fuck off.

Once more, Rip was running. The dead man's guards were firing everywhere, and innocent bystanders, some not so innocent, were dropping like fleas from a poisoned dog. Rip finally got clear of the massacre, though he was twice trampled, kicked in the balls once, and clawed so many times he lost most of his clothes and much of his skin. He was reminded of the one time he'd tallywhacked Brom Dutcher's wife. But now he wasn't getting any pleasure whatsoever.

He ran into a tavern. Panting, he stood by the window and watched the noisy turmoil outside. Then, hearing a small thunderous noise, he turned. Cold ran over him. The noise had been too much like that of the game of ninepins the little old men had played while he drank their Hollands gin, so excellent in taste but so surprising in its effect. He saw some bowling alleys, something new to him. But he paid them no attention. Facing him were two of the little old men. One was the commander, the stout old gentleman in the laced doublet, high-crowned hat, red stockings, and high-heeled shoes.

He spoke in a foreign accent. "It took us some time to track you through time, Rip. Too much of the elixir does more than put you into suspended animation. Anyway, let's go."

"No, no!" Rip said loudly, hoping the patrons would come to his rescue. "Please! This age isn't paradise, but . . ."

This wasn't old New York where everybody's business was yours. No one wanted to get involved now. While the patrons turned away or just watched, the other little man jabbed something into Rip's arm. Unconsciousness fell on him like a mugger.

Just as in the book he'd read, he awoke in A.D. 1792, in the same place where he'd fallen asleep. He had a backache ten times worse than all his hangovers put together. It wasn't from all the fucking he'd done. You couldn't lie on your back without moving for twenty years and not get a backache. Fortunately, the elixir had somehow kept him from freezing to death and had prevented bedsores.

Trudging down to the village, weeping for his lost if half-assed Eden, he thought about the little men. Unlike Washington Irving, Rip didn't think they were the spirits of Henry Hudson and his crew. They were men from outer space, maybe from one of those UFOs that couple had talked about. Or time travelers from the far future.

When Rip got to the village, he knew how to act. Hadn't the scenario been written for him, wouldn't it *be*, rather, by that hack Irving forty-seven years from now? But life wasn't too bad, as it turned out. He was an old man now, fifty-five, and nobody expected him to work for a living. Come to think of it, none but his now departed wife had ever expected it of him. His daughter's husband, a genial fellow, didn't mind supporting him, especially since Rip was now a living legend.

Rip sat often in front of Doolittle's Union Hotel, which had once been van Vedder's Tavern, and he told the story as Irving had, and he got so many free drinks he almost couldn't handle them.

Sometimes, late in the afternoon, loaded with more booze than a rumrunner's ship, he'd close his eyes and doze or seem to doze. The loafers and the tourists around him would see his face clench in fright. They figured he was having a nightmare, and they were right. He was thinking about the bad things in the 20th century, and those would give even the natives of that time nightmares.

Other times, he'd smile, his hips would rotate, and his beard would rise where it covered his fly. Chuckling, snorting, nudging each other's ribs with their elbows, they'd figure that old horny Rip was having a wet dream. They were right, but they didn't know how purple it was.

Osiris on Crutches

I

Set, a god of the ancient land of Egypt, was the first critic. Once he had been a creator, but the people ceased to believe in his creativity. He then suffered a divinity block, which is similar to a writer's block.

This is a sad fate for a deity. Odin and Thor, once cosmic creators, became devils—that is, critics—in the new religion which killed off their old religion. Satan, or Lucifer, was an archangel, in the Book of Job, but he became the chief of demons, the head-honcho critic, in the New Testament. The Great Goddess of the very ancient Mediterranean regions, named Cybele, Anana, Demeter, depending on where she lived, became a demon, Lilith, for instance, or, in one case, the Mother of God (and who criticizes more than a mother?). But she had to do that via the back door, and most people that pray to her don't know that she was not always called Mary. Of course, there are scholars who deny this, just as there are scholars who deny the existence of the Creator.

Those were the days. Gods walked the earth then. They

weren't invisible or absent as they are nowadays. A man or a woman could speak directly to them. They might get only a divine fart in their faces, but if the god felt like talking, the human had a once-in-a-lifetime experience.

Nowadays, you can only get into contact with a god by prayer. This is like sending a telegram which the messenger boy may or may not deliver. And there is seldom a reply by wire, letter, or phone.

In the dawn of mankind, the big gods in Egypt were Osiris, Isis, Nephthys, and Set. They were brothers and sisters, and Osiris was married to Isis and Set was married to Nephthys. Everybody then thought that incest was natural, especially if it took place among the gods.

In any event, no human was dumb enough to protest against the incest. If the gods missed you with their lightning or plagues, the priests got you with their sacrificial knives.

People had no trouble at all seeing the gods, though they might have to be quick about it. The peasants standing in mud mixed with ox manure and the pharaohs standing on their palace porches could see the four great gods, along with Osiris' vizier, Thoth, and Anubis, as they whizzed by. These traveled like the wind or the Roadrunner zooming through the Coyote's traps. Their figures were blurred with speed, dust was their trail, the screaming of split air their only sound.

From dawn to dusk they raced along, blessing the land and all on and in it.

However, the gods noticed a peculiar thing when they roared by a field just north of Abydos. A man always sat in the field, and his back was always turned to them. Sometimes they would speed around to look at his face. But when they did, they still found themselves looking at his back. And if one god went north and one south and one east and one west, four boxing the man in, all four could still only see his back.

"There is One greater than even us," they told each other. "Do you suppose that She, or He, as the case might be, put him there? Or perhaps that is even Him or Her?"

"You mean 'He or She,' " Set said. Even then he was potentially a critic.

After a while they quit staying up nights wondering who the man was and why they couldn't see his face and who put him there. But he was never entirely out of their minds at any time.

There is nothing that bugs an omniscient like not knowing something.

II

Set stopped creating and became a nasty, nay-saying critic because the people stopped believing in him. Gods have vast powers and often use them with no consideration for the feelings or wishes of humans. But every god has a weakness against which he or she or it is helpless. If the humans decide he is an evil god, or a weak god, or a dying god, then he becomes evil or weak or dead. Too bad, Odin! Rotten luck, Zeus! Tough shit, Quetzalcoatl! Trail's end, Gitche Manitou!

But Set was a fighter. He was also treacherous, though he can't be blamed for that since humans had decided that he was no good. He planned some unexpected events for Osiris at the big festival in Memphis honoring Osiris' return from a triumphant world tour, SRO. He planned to shortsheet his elder brother, Osiris, in a big way. From our viewpoint, our six-thousand-year perspective, Set may have had good reason. His sister-wife, Nephthys, was unable to conceive by him and, worse, she lusted after Osiris. Osiris resisted her, though not without getting red in the face and elsewhere.

This was not easy, since Osiris' flesh was green. Which has led some moderns to speculate that he may have come in a flying saucer from Mars. But his flesh was green because that's the color of living plants, and he was the god of agriculture. Among other things.

Nephthys overcame his moral scruples by getting him drunk. (This was the same method used by Lot's daughters many thousands of years later.) The result of this illicit rolling in the reeds was Anubis. Anubis, like a modern immortal, was a "funny-looking kid," and for much the same reason. He had the head of a jackal. This was because jackals ate the dead, and Anubis was the conductor, the ticket-puncher, for the souls who rode into the afterlife.

Bighearted Isis found the baby Anubis in the bulrushes, and she raised him as her own, though she knew very well who the parents were.

Osiris strode into Memphis. He was happy because he had just finished touring the world and teaching non-Egyptians all about peace and nonviolence. The world has never been in such good shape as then and, alas, never will be again. Set smiled widely and spread his arms to embrace Osiris. Osiris should have been wary. Set, as a babe, had torn himself prematurely and violently from his mother's womb, tearing her also. He was rough and wild, white-skinned and red-haired. He was a wild ass of a man.

Isis sat on her throne. She was radiant with happiness. Osiris had been gone for a long time, and she missed him. During his absence, Set had been sidling up to her and asking her if she wanted to get revenge on her husband for his adulterous fling with Nephthys. Isis had told him to beat it. But, truth to tell, she was wondering how long she could have held out. Gods and goddesses are hornier than mere humans, and you know how horny they are.

Isis, however, had to wait. Set gave a banquet that would have turned Cecil B. DeMille green with envy. When everyone ached from stuffing himself, and belches were exploding like rockets over Fort Henry, Set clapped his hands. Four large, but minor, gods staggered in. Among them they bore a marvelously worked coffer. They set it down, and Osiris said, "What is that exquisite *objet d'art*, brother?"

"It's a gift for whomever can fit himself into it exactly," Set said. Anybody else would have said "whoever," but Set was far more concerned with form than content.

To start things off, Set tried to get into the coffer. He was too tall, as he knew he'd be. His seventy-two accomplices in the conspiracy—Set was wicked but he was no piker—were too short. Isis didn't even try. Then Osiris, swaying a little from the gallons of wine he'd drunk, said, "If the coffer fits, wear it." Everybody laughed, and he climbed into the coffer and stretched out. The top of his head just touched the head of the coffer, and the soles of his feet just touched its foot.

Osiris smiled, though not for long. The conspirators slammed the lid down on his face and nailed it down. Set laughed; Isis screamed. The people ran away in panic. Paying no attention to the drumming on the lid from within the coffer, the accomplices rushed the coffer down to the Nile. There they threw it in, and the current carried it seaward.

III

Some gods need air. Others are anaerobic. In those days, they all needed it, though they could live much longer without air than a human could. But it was a long journey down the Nile and across the sea to Byblos, Phoenicia. By the time it grounded on the beach there, Osiris was dead.

Set held Isis prisoner for some time. But Nephthys, who loathed Set now, joined Anubis and Thoth in freeing her. Isis journeyed to Byblos and brought the body back, probably by oxcart, since camels were not yet used. She hid the body in the swamps of a place called Buto. As evil luck would have it, Set was traveling through the swamp, and he fell over the coffer.

His face, when he saw his detested brother's corpse, went through the changes of wood on fire. It became black like wood before the match is applied, then red like flames, than pale like ashes. He tore the corpse into fourteen parts, and he scattered the pieces over the land. He was the destroyer, the spreader of perversity, the venomous nay-sayer.

Isis roamed Egypt looking for Osiris' parts. Tradition has it that she found everything but the phallus. This was supposed to have been eaten by a Nile crab, which is why Nile crabs are forever cursed. But this, like all myths, legends, and traditions, is based on oral material that is inevitably distorted through the ages.

The truth is the crab *had* eaten the genitals. But Isis forced it to disgorge. One testicle was gone, alas. But we know that the myth did not state the truth or at least not all of it. The myth also states that Isis became pregnant with a part of Osiris' body. It doesn't say what part, being vague for some reason. This reason is not delicacy. Ancient myths, in their unbowdlerized forms, were never delicate.

Isis used the phallus to conceive. Presently Horus was born. When he grew up he helped his mother in the search. This took a long time. But they found the head in a mud flat abounding in frogs, the heart on top of a tree, and the intestines being used as an ox whip by a peasant. It was a real mess.

Moreover, Osiris' brain was studded with frog eggs. Every once in a while a frog was hatched. This caused Osiris to have some peculiar thoughts, which led to peculiar behavior. However, if you are a god, or an Englishman, you can get away with eccentricity.

One of the thoughts kicked off by the hatching of a frog egg was the idea of the pyramid. Osiris told a pharaoh about it. The pharaoh asked him what it was good for. Osiris, always the poet, replied that it was a suppository for eternity.

This was true. But he forgot in his poet's enthusiasm his cold scientist's cold regard for cold facts. Eternity has body heat. Everything is slowly oxidizing. The earth and all on it are wrapped in flames if one only has eyes to see them. And so the pyramids, solid though they are, are burning away, falling to pieces. So much for the substantiality of stone.

Meanwhile, Isis and Horus found all of Osiris' body except for a leg and the nose. These seemed lost forever. So she did the best she could. She attached Osiris' phallus to his nose hole.

"After all," she said to Horus and Thoth, "he can wear a kilt to cover his lack of genitals. But he looks like hell without a nose of any kind."

Thoth, the god of writing, and hence also of the short

memory, wasn't so sure. He had the head of an ibis, which was a bird with a very long beak. When Osiris was sexually aroused, he looked too much like Thoth. On the other hand, when Osiris wasn't aroused, he looked like an elephant. Usually, he was aroused. This was because the other gods left him in their dust while he hobbled along on his crutch. But Isis wasn't watching him, and so he dallied with the maidens, and some of the matrons, of the villages and cities along the Nile.

Humans being what they are, the priests soon had him on a schedule which combined the two great loves of mankind: money and sex. He would arrive at 11:45 A.M. at, say, Giza. At 12:00, after the tickets had been collected, he would become the central participant in a fertility rite. At 1:00 the high priest would blow the whistle. Osiris would pick up his crutch and hobble on to the next stop, which was, literally, a whistle stop. The maidens would pick themselves up off the ground and hobble home. Everybody else went back to work.

Osiris met a lot of girls this way, but he had trouble remembering their faces. Just as well. Humans age so fast. He never noticed that the crop of maidens of ten years ago had become careworn, workworn hags. Life was hard then. It was labor before dawn to past dusk, malaria, bilharzia, piles, too much starch and not enough meat and fruit, and, for the women, one pregnancy after another, teeth falling out, belly and breasts sagging, and varicose veins wrapping the legs and the buttocks like sucker vines.

Humans attributed all their ills, of course, to Set. He, they said, was a mean son of a bitch, and when he whirled by, accompanied by tornados, sandstorms, hyenas, and wild asses bearing leaky baskets of bullcrap, life got worse.

They prayed to Osiris and Isis and Horus to get rid of

the primal critic, the basic despoiler. And it happened that Horus did kill him off.

Here's the funny thing about this. Though Set was dead, life for the humans did not get one whit better.

IV

After a few thousand years people caught on to this. They started to quit believing in the ancient Egyptian gods, and so these dwindled away. But the dwindling took time.

Female deities, for some reason, last longer than the males. Isis was worshiped into the sixth century A.D., and when her last temple was closed down, she managed to slip into the Christian church under a pseudonym. Perhaps this is because men and women are very close to their mothers, and Isis was a really big mother.

Osiris, during his wanderings up and down along the Nile, noticed that humans had one method of defeating time. That was art. A man could fix a moment in time forever with a carving or a sculpture or a painting or a poem or a song. The individual passed, nations passed, races passed, but art survived. At least for a while. Nothing is eternal except eternity itself, and even the gods suddenly find that oxidation has burned them down to a crisp.

This is partly because religion is also an art form. And religion, like other art forms, changes with the times.

Osiris knew this, though he hated to admit it to himself. One day, early in the first century A.D., he saw once more the man whose back was always turned to him. This man had been sitting there for about six thousand years or perhaps for much longer. Maybe he was left over from the Old Stone Age.

Osiris decided he'd try once more. He hobbled around on his crutch, circling on the man's left. And then he got a strange burning feeling. The man's face was coming into view.

Straight ahead of the man was what the man's body had concealed. An oblong of blackness the size of a door in a small house lay flat on the earth's surface.

"This is the beginning of the end," Osiris whispered to himself. "I don't know why it is, but I can feel it."

"Greetings, first of the crippled gods, predecessor of Hephaestos and Wieland," the man said. "Ave, first of the gods to be torn apart and then put together again, predecessor of Frey and Lemminkäinen. Hail, first of the gods to die, basic model for those to come, for Baldur and Jesus."

"You don't look like you belong here," Osiris said. "You look like you come from a different time."

"I'm from the twentieth century, which may be the next-to-last century for man or perhaps the last," the man said. "I know what you're thinking, that religion is a form of art. Well, life itself is an art, though most people are imitative artists when it comes to living, painters of the same old paintings over and over again. There are very few originators. Life is a mass art, or usually the art of the masses. And the art of the masses is, unfortunately, bad art. Though often entertaining," he added hastily, as if he feared that Osiris would think he was a snob.

"Who are you?" Osiris said.

"I am Leo Queequeg Tincrowdor," the man said. "Tincrowdor, like Rembrandt, puts himself in his paintings. Any artist worth his salt does. But since I am not worthy to hand Rembrandt a roll of toilet paper, I always paint my back to the viewer. When I become as good as the old Dutchman, I'll show my face in the mob scenes.''

''Are you telling me that you have created me? And all this, too?'' Osiris said. He waved a green hand at the blue river and the pale green and brown fields and the brown and red sands and rocks beyond the fields.

''Every human being knows he created the world when he somehow created himself into being,'' Tincrowdor said. ''But only the artist re-creates the world. Which is why you have had to go through so many millennia with a phallus for a nose and a crutch for a leg.''

''I didn't mind the misplaced phallus,'' Osiris said. ''I can't smell with it, you know, and that is a great benefit, a vast advantage. The world really *stinks*, Tincrowdor. But with this organ up here, I could no longer smell it. So thanks a lot.''

''You're welcome,'' the man said. ''However, you've been around long enough. People have caught on now to the fact that even gods can be crippled. And that crippled gods are symbols of humans and their plight. Humans, you know, are crippled in one way or another. All use crutches, physical or psychical.''

''Tell me something new,'' Osiris said, sneering.

''It's an old observation that will always be new. It's always new because people just don't believe it until it's too late to throw the crutch away.''

Osiris then noticed the paintings half buried in the khaki-, or kaka-, colored dust. He picked them up, blew off the dust, and looked at them. The deepest buried, and so obviously the earliest, looked very primitive. Not Paleolithic but Neolithic. They were stiff, geometrical, awkward, crude, and in garish unnatural colors. In them was Osiris himself and the other deities, two-dimensional, as massive and static as pyramids and hence solid, lacking interior space for interior life. The paintings also had no perspective.

"You didn't know that the world, and hence you, was two-dimensional then, did you?" Tincrowdor said. "Don't feel bad about that. Fish don't know they live in water just as humans don't know a state of grace surrounds them. The difference is, the fish are already in the water, whereas humans have to swim through nongrace to get to the grace."

Osiris looked at the next batch of paintings. Now he was three-dimensional, fluid, graceful, natural in form and color, no longer a stereotype but an individual. And the valley of the Nile had true perspective.

But in the next batch the perspective was lost and he was two-dimensional again. However, somehow, he seemed supported by and integrated with the universe, a feature lacking in the previous batch. But he had lost his individuality again. To compensate for the loss, a divine light shone through him like light through a stained-glass window.

The next set returned to perspective, to three·dimensions, to warm natural colors, to individuality. But, quickly in a bewildering number and diversity, the Nile and he became an abstraction, a cube, a distorted wild beast, a nightmare, a countless number of points confined within a line, a möbius strip, a shower of fragments.

Osiris dropped them back into the dust, and he bent over to look into the oblong of blackness.

"What is that?" he said, though he knew.

"It is," Tincrowdor said, "the inevitable, though not necessarily desired, end of the evolution you saw portrayed in the paintings. It is my final painting. The achievement of pure and perfect harmony. It is nothingness."

Tincrowdor lifted a crutch from the dust which had concealed it all these thousands of years. He did not really need it, but he did not want to admit this to himself. Not yet, anyway—someday, maybe.

Using it as a pole up which to climb, he got to his feet. And, supporting himself on it, he booted the god in the rear. And Osiris fell down and through. Since nothingness is an incomplete equation, Osiris quickly became the other part of the equation—that is, nothing. He was glad. There is nothing worse than being an archetype, a symbol, and somebody else's creation. Unless it's being a cripple when you don't have to be.

Tincrowdor hobbled back to this century. Nobody noticed the crutch—except for some children and some very old people—just as nobody notices a telephone pole until he runs into it. Or a state of grace until it hits him.

As for his peculiarity of behavior and thought—call it eccentricity or originality—this was attributed by everybody to frog eggs hatching in his brain.

St. Francis Kisses His Ass Goodbye

A great mission is made up of many small missions.

Francesco Bernardone, founder in A.D. 1210 of the Friars Minor, the Lesser Brothers, was thinking this as he walked down the steep and winding dirt path halfway up Alverno, a mountain given him by a wealthy admirer. Francesco had refused the gift as a gift; he would not own property, not even his brown woolen robe and the rope used as a belt. He had accepted the mountain as a short-term loan, no interest required.

Behind him ambled the heavily laden ass that was, at the moment, Francesco's small mission, part of a great one. Its nose touched the man in the back now and then, a beast's kiss of affection, though the man had not been near it until he had agreed to take it down to the village for Giovanni the charcoal-burner.

Perhaps the ass also needed to touch its brother, Francesco, for reassurance because the threatening summer storm made it nervous. The dark cloud that always hung near the tip of the peak, though usually brightly rimmed, had swelled like a cobra's hood. Lightning-shot, growling, it was sliding down the firry slopes like a black and fuzzy glacier. The wind was now a hand pushing against his back and snapping the hem of his robe. The storm, like a long-delayed rush of conscience, would soon overtake them; the ass would be terrified by the lightning. Francesco halted and put an arm around the beast's thick neck. Brown eyes looked into a brown eye. The ass's eye was clear with health and innocence; his eyes were clouded with sin and with the disease he had gotten when he had gone to Egypt to convince the Saracens that Jesus was not just one of the prophets, a forerunner, but was unique, the virgin-born son of God, the keeper of the keys to Heaven. He had come back to Italy after the disastrous siege by the Crusaders of Damietta with a great disappointment because his mission had failed, with the friendship of the Saracen king, Malik el-Kamil, and with the malady that blinded him a little more every year and always gave him pain. Brother Pain, who clung to him closer than a blood-brother. And, now that the oncoming clouds had dimmed the light, he could see even less.

He did not know what the ass perceived in his eyes, but he saw one of God's creatures—there were so many, far too many—who needed comfort. Whatever the ass saw, it quit trembling.

"Courage, my brother. If you are struck down, you will be free of your burdens."

Should that happen, he would have to carry the charcoal down the mountain because he had promised Giovanni to deliver the load to the house of Domenico Rivoli, the merchant, and to make sure that someone would bring the ass back up. It would carry food and wine and some money to the burner, his pregnant wife, and his five rib-gaunt children. Francesco could take the charcoal himself, no matter how many trips he had to make, but how could he recompense Giovanni for the animal?

Not one to dwell on possibilities, Francesco plunged on, gripping the ass's halter, and, then, the storm was upon them. He could not see at all. The wind seemed to be trying to tumble him on down the mountain. He was being jerked this way and that by the ass's efforts to tear loose from him. Lightning boomed around him, struck a tree, and dazzled and deafened him. For a moment, he seemed to be sheathed in a bolt, though he knew that he could not have been hit. If he had been, he would not be standing.

Suddenly, he could see. A light from above smote the darkness. It was no lightning. It was a blazing-white spherical mass in which even brighter ribbons turned and lashed out as the mass descended. The ass, braying, trembling again, stood as if transfixed while flame cracked out from its ears, nose, and tail. Sparks and tendrils of brightness shot from Francesco's own body; his fingernails spat fires from their ends.

His lips moving in silent prayer, his eyes shut, he thought that, surely, he was about to be burned alive. Then he opened his eyes. If he was to be burned by the Lord, then that was a martyrdom, and he should see it. Still, this was the first time that God had set one of His own faithful afire. Perhaps, this was like Elijah's being borne by God to Heaven in a fiery chariot. Or was that thought a sinful self-exaltation?

When he closed his eyes again despite telling himself to keep them open, he still saw the light. It seemed to fill his body to the end of his toes. The crash of thunder had ceased. Silence had come with the dazzle. At the same time, he felt a slight tugging—not from the halter— within his body. It was as if he was in the middle of a gigantic and hollow magnet, pulling him from every direction. The attraction was slightly more powerful on one side, but which side he did not know.

Then the halter was jerked from his grip. Though he

was in terror—or was it ecstasy?—he leaped toward where he thought the beast was. He had promised to get it back to Giovanni, and his promises must be fulfilled even when God—or Satan?—had business with him. His hands flailing, one caught the halter. He grabbed the stiff short mane with the other, and, somehow, scrambled up the load until he was on top of it. He felt the pulling on one side of his body grow stronger. It seemed to him, though he could not see anything except the light, that he and the beast were rising. There flashed through his head—a dark thought in the white light filling his skull— that he was like Mahomet who ascended to Heaven on the winged ass, al-Boraq. That story had been told to him by Sultan Malik himself.

But now he was sitting above a cross, the T formed by the pale stripe across the ass's shoulders and down along its spine. In a sense, he was riding the cross that had ridden him most of his life. A great burden he had rejoiced in bearing.

Despite the light, which had not lessened its intensity, he was catching sight of things, brief as lightning flashes but leaving dark, yet somehow burning, afterimages. There was a huge room with many men and women in strange clothes and white coats standing before boxes glowing with many lights and with words in an unknown language, and there were two towering machines in the background which whirled on their axes and shot lightning at each other. That vision was replaced by the dark, big-nosed face of a bearded man in a green turban— something familiar about it—the lips moving with unheard speech. That was gone. Now he saw a great city at night, pulsing with thousands of lights. It was far below him. Pure light banished it. Then it shot out again like a dark jeweled tongue from a mouth formed of light. Now he was closer to it; it was spreading out. Light again. And, once more, the city. He could see buildings with hundreds of well-lit windows, so tall that they would have soared above the Tower of Babel. Enormous machines with stiff unflapping wings flew over them.

He still had the sense of being tugged, though it had suddenly become weaker. He no longer felt airborne. The light was gone. He was in semidarkness. An illumination, feeble compared to that which had filled him, was coming from before him. When he turned his head, he saw a similar illumination behind him. He was in an alley formed by two buildings that went up and up toward a pale night-sky. Around him were a dozen or so figures in bulky clothes. They were staring at this man on the load on top of an ass as if they had appeared out of air, which must be what happened. He was in the middle of a circle formed by a layer of mud six feet across, weeds and bushes sticking at crazy angles out of the dirt which had been transported along with him. He was glad that the air was warm because his robe and he were soaked.

The silence of the journey was gone. The ass was braying loudly; men and women were yelling at him in a foreign language. Now he saw that there were other lights in the alley, flames from the tops of five or six metal barrels spaced out along and next to the two walls. The slight wind brought him odors of long-unwashed bodies and clothes, alcohol, old and fresh piss and shit, decaying teeth, and that stench that rose from the oozing pustules of hopelessness and festering rage.

He was surprised that he could smell all that. He had been immersed in it so long that he scarcely noticed it any more. Perhaps, somehow, his physical and spiritual nostrils had been cleansed during the transit.

Transit to where? This could not be Heaven. Purgatory? Or Hell? He shuddered, then smiled. If, for whatever reason, he had failed to be in God's grace, and there were many reasons why he might have, he could be in

Purgatory or Hell. Come either place, he would have work to do.

His own salvation had never been his main concern, though it was a banked fire in his mind. He had stressed to his disciples that the salvation of others was their mission, that that must be brought about by their examples. If they were to be saved, they must not think about it. It must be done by tending to and taking care of others.

That thought was broken off, a branch snapping, when the dim figures swarmed around him, a mass swelled when others joined it from doorways and packing boxes. Before he could protest, he was hauled roughly from the load and cast painfully upon the pavement. The ass, braying, was pulled down on its side away from Francesco. Knives gleamed in the dull light. The beast tore the night with its death screams as the blades plunged into it. Yelling for them to stop, Francesco got to his feet and began pulling off, or trying to pull off, the men around it. Giving up his efforts, he went to the animal, got down on his knees, and lifted the head, heavy as his heart. He kissed it on its nose, felt it quit shaking, and saw that the open eye was fixed.

The deed was done, and he was grieved, though he would have been glad to give these hungry men the beast to eat if it had been his to give. He had no time to dwell on that. Several men grabbed him and ran their hands over him, then shoved him away with angry exclamations. Apparently, they had been searching for money and valuables. A barefooted man who looked as if Famine and Plague were struggling to determine who would first overcome him, holding a big chunk of blood-dripping meat in one hand and a knife in the other, gestured savagely at him, speaking the tongue Francesco did not know. Hoping that he understood the man's signs, Francesco sat down on the pavement, removed the leather sandals, and handed them to the man.

"Take them with my blessings," Francesco said. He stood up. "If you need my robe, you may have that, too."

The man, scowling, talking to himself, had staggered off to one of the barrels by the side of a building. He threw the meat on a metal grillework on the open top, where it began smoking with the other pieces of meat laid there. The man sat down, wiped his bloodied hands on his coat, and fitted the sandals to his feet. By then, the load had been torn apart and most of it thrown by the barrels or added to the fuel in them.

Francesco stood in the middle of the alley, nauseated not only by the too-swift events but by the feeling that he was hanging by the soles of his feet from an upside-down surface. The city itself seemed to him to have been turned over, and he was hanging like a fly on a ceiling. Yet, when he jumped slightly to reassure his confused senses that he was not kept from falling by a glue on the bottom of his feet, he came back to the pavement as quickly as he always had.

When he saw some monstrous white thing with two glowing eyes that shot beams of light ahead of it, speeding on the street at the end of the alley, he ignored his nausea and started toward the street. Before he got there, two more of the frightening things went by. But he saw the people within them and knew that they were some kind of self-propelled vehicle. He clung to the corner of the building while others shot by. Was he in a city of wizards and witches? If so, he must indeed be in Hell.

There was more to add to his bewilderment. The buildings along the street were fronted with gigantic panels on which icons of people and animals flashed and many words sprang into light and then disappeared. His mind swirling like the strange many-colored geometric patterns on some of the panels, he stepped back into the alley. He would speak to each of the people there and determine if any spoke Umbrian or Roman Italian or Latin or Provençal, or if any could understand the limited phrases he knew of Arabic, Berber, Aragonese, Catalan, Greek, Turkish, German or English.

He stopped, rigid at the sight of a black woman who was on her knees and holding with one hand the swollen penis of the white man standing above her while she moved her head back and forth along the shaft in her mouth. Her other hand supported a baby sucking at her nipple. In the man's hand was a piece of half-cooked meat. Her payment?

Before Francesco could recover, he heard a loud up-and-down wailing, and a huge vehicle screeched around the corner, making him dive to escape being struck. It stopped, its two beams making noon out of the twilight in the alley, blue and red lights on it flashing, the wailing it made dying down. The man pulled loose from the woman's mouth and ran toward a doorway. Some of the others fled from the barrels; some froze. Doors in the side and rear of the vehicle snapped out and down. Men and women in bright blue uniforms, wearing blue helmets, and holding what had to be weapons, though of a nature that Francesco did not know, sprang shouting from its interior. He, with the other alley people, was shoved with his face against the wall, his outstretched hands against the wall, his legs spread out. He looked around and was cuffed alongside his head with the barrel of a weapon.

But he looked again anyway, and he saw another huge machine, its front a great open mouth, lumber past the first vehicle. It stopped short of the carcass, waited while some uniforms pointed small flashing boxes at the dead ass, then scooped it up with a long broad metal tongue and drew it into the dark maw. The uniforms kicked over the barrels so that the fiery fuel and meat spilled onto the pavement. After this, the uniforms questioned the denizens of the alley but got very little response except some obvious cursing. Francesco could not answer his interrogator, but the uniform just laughed and passed on to the next man. Francesco turned around and, once more, was shocked, this time so much that he was unable for a moment to think coherently.

Three of the alley men were in a stage of activity at a point where they could or would not stop. A man was buggering a tall and very skinny man whose lower garment was around his ankles. He had whiskers that radiated around his face, and in the center of the whiskers was the penis of a man standing before the whiskery man, sliding back and forth rapidly. The uniforms had not touched or questioned them. Evidently, they regarded the spectacle as comic because those standing around were laughing and jeering. But, just as two of the men were screaming with ecstasy, the round top of the second vehicle pointed a long metal tube at the trio, and water shot out of its end. The three were knocked down and rolled over and over until they collided violently with a wall.

The uniforms laughed, then became grim. After the alley people, Francesco among them, had been forced to set the barrels upright again, the hose on top of the machine washed the charcoal and the fuel and the pieces of meat and other trash down the alley until the mass was swallowed by an opening below the curb at the end of the alley. Many of the alley people were struck by the jet.

This distressed Francesco more than anything he had so far seen. It was a great sin to deny food to these hungry unfortunates.

Brother Sun arose a few minutes after the uniforms and their vehicles had left. Cold from the double-soaking despite the warm air, cold also from the transit and the aftermath, very bewildered, Francesco shivered. Not until day had worn on and the air had become hot did he stop quaking. By then, the alley people, looking even more tired, haggard, ugly, and hungry, had dispersed. Later, he would see several of them begging for money. He left the alley to walk on the sidewalk northward through the canyon street. The vehicles, scarce at first, soon became numerous. They jammed the streets as they crawled along, and their honking never stopped. By noon, when people swarmed on the sidewalks, an acrid odor which he had noticed about mid-morning became heavy, and his eyes burned. Then Brother Sun was covered up by his sister clouds. Despite this, the breeze became hotter.

Becoming ever more hungry, he tried vainly to stop some of the pedestrians to beg for bread. They were well-fed and luxuriously dressed, though the clothes of some of the women exposed so much that he was embarrassed. After a while, he got used to that. But his pleas for food were still ignored. He also encountered many crazed people, some beggars, some not, who talked to themselves or shouted loudly at others. These, however, had also populated his own world; he was used to them.

He passed a large building with many broad steps leading up to it and two large stone lions set halfway up the staircase. On the sidewalk near it he stopped by a cart from behind which a man sold food the like of which he had never seen before. Its odors made his mouth water. A man bought a paper sack full of some small puffy white balls and began scattering them for the pigeons abounding here. Francesco asked him for some of the white stuff, but the man turned his back on him.

Passing on, he saw glass-fronted restaurants crammed with customers stuffing themselves. He entered one and got the attention of a servant behind the counter by pointing to his open mouth and rubbing his stomach. A big man grabbed him by the back of his robe and forced him violently, though Francesco did not struggle or protest, back onto the sidewalk.

His belly rumbled. So did the thunder westward. The skies were now black, and the breeze had become a wind that rippled the hems of his robe. It was beginning to cool, though, and the stink that burned his eyes was lessening. The tugging inside him and the feeling of being upside down were still with him, present when he was not too absorbed in the strangeness. He turned to the west and walked until he came to a river. Though thirsty, he did not drink from it. He had often drunk from water that had a bad odor, but this was too strong for him. He went north, then west, then south, then west again, and came to another river, equally malodorous. On both shores were elevated highways, jammed with the ever-honking vehicles. The whole city was a din.

Now he did what many of the unfortunates were doing, opening garbage cans and searching therein. He found a half-eaten semicircle of a baked crust of dough with pieces of some strange red vegetable and of meat mixed with cheese. The box underneath it had printed words on it. One of them was PIZZA. Derived from *picca*, meaning *pie*? He devoured that, though it was dry and hard, then dug up another half-eaten item made up of two slices of hard and moldy bread in the middle of which was meat beginning to stink. Nevertheless, he started to bite down on that when a stray dog stopped by him and looked pleadingly at him. Its mangy skin covered a body that seemed more skeleton than flesh. He tossed the bread and meat to the dog, who bolted it. Francesco petted the dog. After that, it followed him for a while but deserted him to investigate an overturned garbage can.

Despite not knowing any of the languages he overheard during his journey through the upside-down city, Francesco had made many interpretations by mid-noon.

There were other languages than those issuing from mouths. For instance, the tongue of the city itself, the tongue composed of many tongues just as a great mission was composed of many small ones. Cities were the first machines built by man, social machines, true, but Francesco was especially adept at translating the unspoken languages of cities. The architecture, the artifacts, the art, the music, the traffic, the manners, the expressions of faces and voices, the subtle and the not-so-subtle body movements, the distribution of goods and food, the ways in which the keepers of the law and the breakers of the law (often they were the same) behaved toward each other and toward the citizens upon whom they preyed and who preyed on them, these all formed a great machine which was part organism and part mechanical.

God certainly knew, as did Francesco, that there were enough mechanical artifacts in this city to have provided all of the world that he knew with plenty of them. Aside from the vehicles, there were the blaring mechanical voices in every store and on every street corner and there were the moving and flashing icons that covered the fronts of buildings and were in unnumberable numbers inside the buildings. He did not know the purpose of most. But he understood that the flat cases people wore strapped to their wrists were used to talk at a distance with others and that the many booths on the sidewalks were used for the same purpose.

The whole city was, among other things, a message center. But did these men and women understand the messages, the truth behind the words and images? Did they care if they understood correctly? Did the devices widen the doors for the entrance of the truth? Or did they widen the doors for more lies to enter? Or did they do both?

If both, then the result was that these people were more confused than those of his world. Too much information combined with the inability to separate truth from falsehood was as bad as ignorance. Especially when the disseminators of lies claimed that these were truths. Just as he concluded this, Francesco saw the gaunt man with the whiskery halo-fringe, the buggeree and sucker who had been interrupted in the alley by the uniforms. He was sitting on the sidewalk with his back against a building wall. Francesco could see the scabs, pustules, and blotches covering his face, arms, and the bony legs. He could also see that indefinable expression of the slowly dying. But it was changing into that of those who would soon be able to express nothing. Francesco had seen that too many times not to recognize it.

Now he knew that he was neither in Purgatory or Hell. Whatever else there was in those places, death was not there.

Francesco made his way through the throng, all of whom were ignoring the man, some of whom stepped over his bare legs. He knelt by the man and took his sore-covered hand. It was almost as fleshless as Brother Death's himself. Francesco, though he knew he would not be understood, asked what he could do for him? Did he need to be carried to a sickhouse? Was he hungry? His questions were intended to make the man comprehend that he was with someone who cared for him. There was really nothing that Francesco could do to stave off the irresistible.

The man leaned forward and mumbled something. Francesco took him in his arms and held him while the man's mouth moved against the robe. What was he trying to say? It sounded like *priest*. Suddenly, Francesco knew that the word was some kind of English, though certainly not what he had learned from Brother Haymo of Faversham, his English disciple.

"Prete! Prete!" Francesco said.

For the first time in his life, Francesco felt helpless.

He had always been able to do something for those who needed help, but he could not make anyone understand what needed doing now, and he himself could do nothing.

The wind lashed out, even more cool now, and the thunder was closer. A few raindrops fell on his head. Lightning chainlinked the clouds. Then, the blackening clouds tipped over barrels of rain. He and the man were soaked, and the sidewalk was quickly emptied of all but himself and the man he held in his arms. That did not matter since they would not have helped him anyway.

He prayed, "O Lord, this man wishes to confess, to repent, and to be forgiven. Is not the intent good enough for You? What does it matter if no priest is here to hear him? I do not hate him, no matter what he has done. I love him. If I, a more mortal, one of Your creatures, can love him, how much more must You!"

"He is gone," a deep melodious voice said. Francesco turned his head and looked up through the water blurring his already dimmed vision. As if there were a mirage before him—a dry desert phenomenon beneath the surface of the sea—he saw standing by him a tall man in a green robe and wearing a green turban. Francesco gently released the sagging corpse, wiped the rain from his eyes with his wet sleeve, and stood close to the man. He started. The face was that of the man whom he had glimpsed while in transit to this place. It was handsome and hawk-nosed, its eyebrows thick and dark, looking like transplanted pieces of a lion's mane. The leaf-green eyes in the almost black face were startling.

"It was not easy finding you," the man said. Francesco started again. He had not realized until now that the man was speaking in Provençal.

"Others are looking for you," the man said. "They are frantic to find you, but they do not know what you look like and so will fail. In fact, they do not know if they have transported a man or a woman or an animal or some combination of these. But their indicators make them think that they have picked up at least one human being, possibly more. Unless someone else does for them what they cannot do, they will be responsible for an explosion which will considerably change the face of Earth and might kill all humans and much of the higher forms of animals. We have approximately three hours to prevent this event. If Allah wills . . .''

So, the man was a Muslim. That thought overrode for a moment the prediction of the cataclysm. Francesco started to ask a question, but the man continued.

''They did not know this would happen until immediately after they had transported you. Their . . .'' He paused, then said, ''You would not understand the word. Their . . . thinking machine . . . gave a false result because of a slight mathematical error put into the machine by the operator. Slight but reverberating greatly . . . swelling. To prevent an explosion of any degree, they must send you back. Not only you but all that came with you. That is impossible, but the effect may be considerably reduced if they send back not only you but a mass approximating that which was brought along with you. You will have to estimate that mass for them, describe what did come in with you.''

The man stepped into the street and held a hand up. A black vehicle skidded to a stop a few inches before the man. He went to the front left-side window and spoke to the man seated there. A very angry-looking man and woman got out of the back seat a minute later. The green-turbaned man gestured to Francesco to come quickly. Francesco got into the back seat next to him. The vehicle's wheels screamed as it leaped like a rabbit that had just seen a fox. The man spoke a few short words of what had to be English into the small case strapped to his wrist. Numbers flashed on its top.

"There will be no more time travel experiments," the man said. "The data . . . the information . . . has been sent secretly to the government of this country and to those of all nations. The populaces will not be informed until after the explosion, if then. Notifying the people of this city would only cause a panic, and the city could not possibly be evacuated. Even if it could be, the people could not get far enough away unless they went in an airplane . . . a flying machine. And only a few could get away in time. The people in the project are staying. They will work until the explosion comes, and they hope that its effects will be considerably reduced, as I said, by sending you back."

Francesco, clinging to a strap above the door, said, "Are you telling me that I have somehow been plucked by satanic powers from my time to a future time?"

"Yes, though the powers are not satanic. Their effect may be, though."

The man pointed out the window by Francesco at a building Francesco could see dimly. But he could make out a tall structure with many spires on the upper half of which was a gigantic panel. Its upper third flashed orange letters, one forming FRANCIS. The lower two-thirds displayed a bright and strange figure, a six-winged and crucified seraph surrounded by roiling light-purple clouds, which in turn were surrounded by swirling, fast-changing, and many-colored geometric figures. Then the vehicle was past it.

"A Catholic church, SAINT FRANCIS OF THE POOR. Attended mainly by the rich." The man chuckled, and he said, "Dedicated to you, Francesco Bernardone of Assisi."

Francesco, who had always felt at ease when events were going too swiftly for others to comprehend, was now numb.

"I was canonized?"

"Yes, but your order started to depart from your ideals, to decay, as it were, before your corpse was cold. Or so it was said."

Francesco bit his lower lip until the blood came, and he dug his fingernails into the palms of his hands until they felt like iron nails being driven in.

"I will *not* change."

"Because you know this? No, you will not."

"When did I die?"

"It would be wise for you not to know."

"But I am going back. Otherwise . . ."

"Obviously. But what happens here after you do . . . that is another matter. The force of the explosion caused by the interaction of matter and temporal energy will be proportional to the amount left here of the matter you brought with you. If, for example, you had held your breath during the transit, then expelled after arriving here, the amount of expelled air—if confined to a small area, and it won't be—would be enough to blow up that church and several blocks around it. What the project people need to know is just how much matter you did bring with you."

Francesco told him what had come in with him and what had happened to it.

"Your sandals, the urine you've pissed out, the dirt surrounding you, the plants and insects in the dirt, the body of the ass left after the butchering, the pieces of meat cooking on the barrels, the smoke from them, and the meat in the bodies of the men who ate it should go back with you. But, of course, they can't. You'll have to estimate an equivalent mass from your memory. The mass can't be exact, but if it's anything near that which was brought in, it will help cancel some of the effects of the mass-temporal energy explosion."

The man thought for a moment. He said, "After I deliver you, I will leave this area. Even I . . . no time for that now. The northeastern coast will be destroyed and much of the interior country. Many millions will die. But the world will go on.''

Francesco said, ''You seem to know so much. Why didn't you stop them? At least, warn them.''

''I knew no more than they did what would happen. There is only One who is all-wise. I had nothing to do with the project, though I was well informed about it. I was not supposed to be, which is why they were so outraged and furious when I called in and told them I would search for you. They will try to arrest me when I bring you in, though that is stupid because I would be blown to bits along with them. They will not be able to hold me, and you will go back. The world knows when you died. So it is written that you return to your time.''

''Not without the ass . . . an ass,'' Francesco said.

''What?''

Francesco told him of his promise to Giovanni, the charcoal-burner. ''And there must be a load of charcoal, too.''

The man spoke again to the case on his wrist, listened, spoke again, listened, then said, ''They find it hard to believe that you would rather let the east coast blow up than go back without the donkey. I told them that I doubted that, but it would go easier and faster if they did what you want.''

''Is it difficult to obtain an ass and charcoal?''

''No. The ass will come from a nearby zoo . . . a place where animals are kept. It should arrive soon even if it has to be airlift . . . brought in a flying machine.'' He smiled and said, ''I told them they should get the biggest ass possible. I suggested that they might substitute the head of the project if for some reason they couldn't get one at the zoo. He fits all your qualifications, aside from being bipedal and lacking long ears.''

"Thank you. However, I do not like to go back without even knowing your name."

"Here I am called Kidder."

"Elsewhere . . . it's not Elijah?"

"I have many names. Some of them are appropriate." Francesco wondered why he had seen Kidder's face during the transit. The forces that had shot him from there to here must have been connected with some psychic—or supernatural—phenomena even if the people who were running the project did not know that. His question, however, was forgotten when the vehicle was caught in slow-moving traffic that did not speed up no matter how long and hard the driver blew the horn. The man talked into his wrist-case again, and, within two minutes, a flying machine appeared at a low altitude above them. It descended, pods on its sides burning at their lower end and emitting a frightening and deafening noise. It landed on a sidewalk, and Francesco and Kidder got into it and were whisked up and away. By then, Francesco was so frozen that he was not scared. The machine landed on top of a high building. He and Kidder got out and were ushered swiftly to an elevator that plunged downwards and stopped suddenly, and then they were hustled along by many white-coated men and women and some uniforms to a great room filled with many machines with flashing lights and fleeting icons and numbers.

Francesco was placed in the center of the room inside a circle marked on the floor. An ass with a burden of charcoal, a large handsome beast, so much better than the poor one that had come with him that he would have to tell Giovanni not to ask questions about it, just be grateful and thank God for it, was led in.

Francesco, this throat dry, said huskily, "*Signore* Kidder, satisfy my curiosity. What is today's date?"

"Seven hundred and eighty years after your birth," Kidder said. And he was gone, somehow removing himself from the crowd around him and the two uniforms who stood behind him. Francesco cried out to him that he remembered now where he had seen him before the transit. He had been in the camp of Sultan Malik, where Francesco had glimpsed him a few times but had not thought that he was more than one of the Sultan's court. Kidder probably had not heard him. Even if he had been in the crowd, he would not have caught Francesco's words. The two uniforms were shouting too loudly as they tried to force their way through the crowd in search of Kidder.

Then bags of dirt were stacked alongside him and the ass in the center of the circle, and the workers withdrew. The crowd moved back to the walls of the room. They all looked haggard and frightened and white-faced. Francesco felt sorry for them because they knew that they were doomed no matter what happened to him. He blessed them and prayed for them and blessed them again.

The lights flickered; a terrible whining pierced his ears and skull. A great ball of swirling white light descended from a conelike device in the ceiling. It surrounded him, and, though he cried out, he could not hear his own voice. The tugging sensation that had never left him became stronger. He was once more in that limbo in which he saw dimly, again, the men and women in the building and the turbaned head of Kidder.

Then he was in rain and thunder, and the ass was braying loudly beside him. Under his feet was a very thin section of the floor inside the circle.

He no longer felt the tugging, and the world no longer seemed upside down.

It was not long after this that Francesco saw on Mount Alverno the vision of the six-winged and crucified seraph in the skies and that Francesco was blessed—or cursed—with the marks of the nails in his hands (which he tried to conceal as much as possible). And then, seemingly as swift as that transit of which he never spoke, the time came when he was dying. The brothers and sisters were gathered around him, speaking softly, church bells were ringing, and, outside the hut, the rich and the powerful and the poor were standing, praying for him. His blinded eyes were open as if he could see what the others could not, which indeed he could. He was wondering if the seraph he had seen on the panel on the church front during that wild ride had possibly influenced him, caused him to envision that aweful, painful, yet ecstatic flying figure above the mountain.

Which had come first? His seeing the seraph on that panel in the far future or the splendor in the sky? He would never know. The mysteries of time were beyond him—at this moment.

He wondered about Kidder. Could he be that mysterious Green Man Francesco had heard about from some wise men of the East? He was supposed to have been the secret counsellor of Moses and of many others, and he showed up now and then, here and there, when the need for him was great. But that implied . . .

That thought faded as another Francesco, an almost transparent Francesco, rose like smoke from his body and stood there looking down at him. Its lips moved, but he could not hear its voice. It kneeled down by him and bent over. Now, he could read the lips.

"Goodbye, Brother Ass," he, the other, said. His body, that creature that he had treated so hard, driven so unmercifully, and to which he had apologized more than once for the burdens he had heaped on it, that was leaving him. No, he was leaving it. Now, he was looking down upon his own dead face. He leaned over and kissed its lips and stood up, happy as never before, and he had always been filled with joy even when hungry and wet and cold and longing vainly for others to have his happiness.

He was ready for whatever might come but hoped that he would have work to do.

Not like that on Earth.

The Oögenesis
of Bird City

The President of the U.S.A. sat at the desk of the mayor of Upper Metropolitan Los Angeles, Level 1. There was no question of where the mayor was to sit. Before the office of mayor could be filled, the electorate had to move into the city.

The huge room was filled with U.S. cabinet heads and bureau chiefs, senators, state governors, industrial and educational magnates, union presidents, and several GIP presidents. Most of them were watching the TV screens covering one part of the curving wall.

Nobody looked through the big window behind the President, even though this gave a view of half of the city. Outside the municipal building, the sky was blue with a few fleecy clouds. The midsummer sun was just past the zenith, yet the breeze was cool; it was 73°F everywhere in the city. Of the 200,000 visitors, at least one-third were collected around tourguides. Most of the hand-carried football-sized TV cameras of the reporters were focused at the moment on one man.

Government spieler: "Ladies 'n gentlemen, you've been personally conducted through most of this city and you now know almost as much as if you'd stayed home and watched it on TV. You've seen everything but the interior of the houses, the inside of your future homes. You've been amazed at what Uncle Sam, and the state of California, built here, a Utopia, an Emerald City of Oz, with you as the Wizard . . ."

Heckler (a large black woman with an M.A. in Elementary School Electronic Transference): "The houses look more like the eggs that Dorothy used to frighten the Nome King with!"

Spieler (managing to glare and smile at the same time): "Lady, you've been shooting your mouth off so much, you must be an agent for the Anti-Bodies! You didn't take the pauper's oath; you took the peeper's oath!"

Heckler (bridling): "I'll sue you for defamation of character and public ridicule!"

Spieler (running his gaze up and down her whale-like figure): "Sue, sue, sooie! No wonder you're so sensitive about eggs, lady. There's something ovoid about you!"

The crowd laughed. The President snorted disgustedly and spoke into a disc strapped to his wrist. A man in the crowd, the message relayed through his ear plug, spoke into his wrist transmitter, but the spieler gestured as if to say, "This is my show! Jump in the lake if you don't like it!"

Spieler: "You've seen the artificial lake in the center of the city with the municipal and other buildings around it. The Folk Art Center, the Folk Recreation Center, the hospital, university, research center, and the PANDORA, the people's all-necessities depot of regulated abundance. You've been delighted and amazed with the fairyland of goodies that Uncle Sam, and the State of California, offers you free. Necessities and luxuries, too, since *Luxury Is A Necessity*, to quote the FBC. You want anything—anything!—you go to the PANDORA, press some buttons, and presto! you're rich beyond your dreams!''

Heckler: "When the lid to Pandora's box was opened, all the evils in the world flew out, and . . .''

Spieler: "No interruptions, lady! We're on a strict time schedule . . .''

Heckler: "Why? We're not going anyplace!''

Spieler: "I'll tell you where you can go, lady.''

Heckler: "But . . .''

Spieler: "But me no buts, lady. You know, you ought to go on a diet!''

Heckler (struggling to control her temper): "Don't get personal, big mouth! I'm big, all right, and I got a wallop, too, remember that. Now, Pandora's box . . .''

The spieler made a vulgar remark, at which the crowd laughed. The heckler shouted but could not be heard above the noise.

The President shifted uneasily. Kingbrook, the 82-year-old senator from New York, harumphed and said, "The things they permit nowadays in the public media. Really, it's disgusting . . .''

Some of the screens on the wall of the mayor's office showed various parts of the interior of the city. One screen displayed a view from a helicopter flying on the oceanside exterior of Upper Metropolitan LA. It was far enough away to get the entire structure in its camera, including the hundred self-adjusting cylinders that supported the Brobdingnagian plastic cube and the telescoping elevator shafts dangling from the central underbase. Beneath the shadow of box and legs was the central section of the old city and the jagged sprawl of the rest of Los Angeles and surrounding cities.

The President stabbed towards the screen with a cigarette and said, "Screen 24, gentlemen. The dark past below. The misery of a disrupted ant colony. Above it, the bright complex of the future. The chance for everyone to realize his full potentiality as a human being."

Spieler: "Before I conduct you into this house, which is internally just like every other private residence . . ."

Heckler: "Infernally, you mean. They all look just alike on the outside, too."

Spieler: "Lady, you're arousing my righteous wrath. Now, folks, you noticed that all the buildings, municipal and private, are constructed like eggs. This futuristic design was adopted because the egg shape, according to the latest theory, is that of the universe. No corners, all curving, infinity within a confined space, if you follow me."

Heckler: "I don't!"

Spieler: "Take off a little weight, lady, and you'll be in shape to keep up with the rest of us. The ovoid form gives you a feeling of unbounded space yet of security-closeness. When you get inside . . ."

Every house was a great smooth white plastic egg lifted 18.28 meters above the floor of the city by a thick truncated-cone support. (Offscreen commentators explained that 18.18 meters was 20 feet, for the benefit of older viewers who could not adjust to the new system of measurement.) On two sides of the cone were stairs ending at a horizontal door on the lower side of the ovoid. These opened automatically to permit entrance. Also, a door opened in the cone base, and an elevator inside lifted the sick or crippled or, as the spieler put it, "the just plain lazy, everybody's got a guaranteed right to be lazy." The hollow base also housed several electrical carts for transportation around the city.

The President saw Kierson, the Detroit automobile magnate, frown at the carts. The auto industry had shifted entirely from internal combustion motors to electrical and nuclear power ten years ago, and now Kierson saw the doom of these. The President made a mental note to pacify and reassure him on this point later.

Spieler: ". . . *Variety Within Unity*, folks. You've heard a lot about that on FBC, and these houses are an example. In reply to the lady's anxiety about the houses all looking alike, every home owner can paint the outside of his house to express his individuality. Anything goes. From reproductions of Rembrandt to psychedelic dreams to dirty words, if you got the guts. Everything's free, including speech . . ."

Heckler: "They'll look like a bunch of Easter eggs!"

Spieler: "Lady, Uncle Sam *is* The Big Easter Bunny!"

The spieler took the group into the house, and the cameramen went into the atrium, kitchen, and the ten rooms to show the viewers just what the citizens-to-be were getting for nothing.

"For nothing!" Senator Kingbrook growled. "The taxpayers are paying through the nose, through every orifice, with their sweat and blood for this!"

The President said, mildly, "They won't have to in the future, as I'll explain."

"You don't have to explain anything to any of us," Kingbrook said. "We all know all about the economy of abundance versus the economy of scarcity. And about your plans for the transitional stage, which you call ORE, *obverse-reverse* economy, but which I call *schizophrenic horrors in tremens*!"

The President smiled and said, "You'll have your say, Senator."

The men and women in the room were silent for a while as they watched the spieler extol the splendors and virtues of the house with its soundproof walls, the atrium with its pool, the workshop with machinery for crafts, the storeroom, the bedroom-studios, TV in every room, *retractable* and inflatable furniture, air-conditioning, microfilm library, and so on.

Government shill: "This is fabulous! A hell of a lot better than any noisy rat-ridden dump on the ground!"

Spieler (quoting an FBC slogan): "*Happy and free as the birds in the air!* That's why everybody calls this Bird City and why the citizens are known as freebirds! Everything first class! Everything free!"

Heckler: "Except freedom to live where you want to in the type of house you want!"

Spieler: "Lady, unless you're a millionaire, you won't be able to get a house on the ground that isn't just like every other house. And then you'd have to worry about it being burned down. Lady, you'd gripe if you was hung with a new rope!"

The group went outside where the spieler pointed out that, though they were three hectometers above ground, they had trees and grass in small parks. If they wanted to fish or boat, they could use the lake in the municipal-building area.

Shill: "Man, this is living!"

Spieler: "The dome above the city looks just like the sky outside. The sun is an electronic reproduction; its progress exactly coincides with that of the real sun. Only, you don't have to worry about it getting too cold or too hot in here or about it raining. We even got birds in here."

Heckler: "What about the robins? Come springtime, how're they going to get inside without a pass?"

Spieler: "Lady, you got a big mouth! Whyn't you . . ."

The President rose from his chair. Kingbrook's face was wrinkled, fissured, and folded with old age. The red of his anger made his features look like hot lava on a volcano slope just after an eruption. His rich rumble pushed against the eardrums of those in the room as if they were in a pressure chamber.

"A brave new concentration camp, gentlemen! Fifty billion dollars worth to house 50,000 people! The great bankruptopolis of the future! I estimate it'll cost one trillion dollars just to enclose this state's population in these glorified chicken runs!''

"Not if ORE is put into effect,'' the President said. He held up his hand to indicate silence and said, "I'd like to hear Guildman, gentlemen. Then we can have our conferences.''

Senator Beaucamp of Mississippi muttered, "One trillion dollars! That would house, feed, and educate the entire population of my state for twenty years!''

The President signalled to cut off all screens except the FBC channel. The private network commentators were also speaking, but the federal commentator was the important one. His pitch was being imitated—if reluctantly—by the private networks. Enough pressure and threats had been applied to make them wary of going all-out against the President. Although the mass media had been restrained, the speech of private persons had not been repressed. For one thing, the public needed a safety valve. Occasionally, a private speaker was given a chance to express himself on TV and radio. And so, a cavalry charge of invectives had been and was being hurled at the President. He had been denounced as an ultra-reactionary, a degenerate liberal, a Communist, a Fascist, a vulture, a pig, a Puritan, a pervert, a Hitler, etc., and had been hung *in absentia* to many times that an enterprising manufacturer of effigies had made a small fortune—though taxes made it even smaller.

From cavalry to Calvary, he thought. All charges admitted. All charges denied. I am human, and that takes in everything. Even the accusation of fanaticism. I know that what I'm doing is right, or, at least, the only known way. When the Four Horsemen ride, the countercharge cannot be led by a self-doubter.

The voice of the Great Guildman, as he was pleased to be called, throbbed through the room. Chief FBC commentator, bureau executive, Ph.D. in Mass Communications, G-90 rating, one who spoke with authority, whose personal voltage was turned full-on, who could, some said, have talked God into keeping Adam and Eve in the garden.

". . . cries out! The people, the suffering earth itself, cry out! The air is poisoned! The water is poisoned! The soil is poisoned! Mankind is poisoned with the excess of his genius for survival! The wide walls of the Earth have become narrowed! Man, swelling like a tumor with uncontrolled growth, kills the body that gave him birth! He is squeezing himself into an insane mold which crushes his life out, crushes all hope for an abundant life, security, peace, quiet, fulfillment, dignity . . ."

The audience, tuning in on forty channels, was well aware of this; he was painting a picture the oils of which had been squeezed from their own pain. And so Guildman did not tarry overlong at these points. He spoke briefly of the dying economy of scarcity, obsolete in the middle 1900's but seeming vigorous, like a sick man with a fatal disease who keeps going on larger and larger shots of drugs and on placebos. Then he splashed bright colors over the canvas of the future.

Guildman went on about the population expansion, automation, the ever-growing permanently depressed class and its riots and insurrections, the ever-decreasing and ever-overburdened taxpayers with their strikes and riots, the Beverly Hills Massacre, the misery, crime, anger, etc.

The President repressed an impulse to squirm. There would be plenty of blacks and grays in The Golden World (the President's own catch-phrase). Utopia could never exist. The structure of human society, in every respect, had a built-in instability, which meant that there would always be a certain amount of suffering and maladjustment. There were always victims of change.

But that could not be helped. And it was a good thing that change was the unchanging characteristic of society. Otherwise, stagnation, rigidity, and loss of hope for improvement would result.

Beaucamp leaned close to the President and said softly, "Plenty of people have pointed out that the economy of abundance eventually means the death of capitalism. You've never commented on this, but you can't keep silent much longer."

"When I do speak," the President said, "I'll point out that EOA also means the death of socialism and communism. Besides, there's nothing sacred in an economic system, except to those who confuse money with religion. Systems are made for man, not vice versa."

Kingbrook rose from his sofa, his bones cracking, and walked stiffly towards the President.

"You've rammed through this project despite the opposition of the majority of taxpayers! You used methods that were not only unconstitutional, sir! I know for a fact that criminal tactics were used, blackmail and intimidation, sir! But you will go no more on your Caesar's road! This project has beggared our once wealthy nation, and we are not going to build any more of your follies! Your grandiose—and wicked—Golden World will be as tarnished as brass, as green as fool's gold, by the time that I am through with you! Don't underestimate me and my colleagues, sir!"

"I know of your plans to impeach me," the President said with a slight smile. "Now, Senators Beaucamp and Kingbrook, and you, Governor Corrigan, would you step into the mayor's apartment? I'd like to have a few words— I hope they're few—with you."

Kingbrook, breathing heavily, said, "My mind is made up, Mr. President. I know what's wrong and what's right for our country. If you have any veiled threats or insidious proposals, make them in public, sir! In this room, before these gentlemen!''

The President looked at the embarrassed faces, the stony, the hostile, the gleeful, and then glanced at his wristwatch. He said, "I only ask five minutes."

He continued, "I'm not slighting any of you. I intend to talk to all of you in groups selected because of relevant subjects. Three to five minutes apiece will let us complete our business before the post-dedication speeches. Gentlemen!" And he turned and strode through the door.

A few seconds passed, and then the three, stiff-faced, stiff-backed, walked in.

"Sit down or stand as you please," the President said.

There was a silence. Kingbrook lit a cigar and took a chair. Corrigan hesitated and then sat near Kingbrook. Beaucamp remained standing. The President stood before them.

He said, "You've seen the people who toured this city. They're the prospective citizens. What is their outstanding common characteristic?"

Kingbrook snorted and said something under his breath. Beaucamp glared at him and said, "I didn't hear your words, but I know what you said! Mr. President, I intend to speak loudly and clearly about this arrogant discrimination! I had one of my men run the list of accepted citizens through a computer, and he reports that the citizens will be 100 percent Negro! And 7/8ths are welfares!"

"The other eighth are doctors, technicians, teachers, and other professionals," the President said. "All volunteers. There, by the way, goes the argument that no one will work if he doesn't have to. These people will be living in this city and getting no money for their labor. We had to turn down many volunteers because there was no need for them."

"Especially since the government has been using public funds to brainwash us with the Great-Love-and-Service-for-Humanity campaign for twenty years,'' Kingbrook said.

"I never heard you making any speeches knocking love or service,'' the President said. ''However, there is another motive which caused so many to offer their services. Money may die out, but the desire for prestige won't. The wish for prestige is at least as old as mankind itself and maybe older.''

"I can't believe that no whites asked to live here,'' Beaucamp said.

"The rule was, first apply, first accepted,'' the President said. "The whole procedure was computer-run, and the application blanks contained no reference to race.''

Corrigan said, "You know that computers have been gimmicked or their operators bribed.''

The President said, "I am sure that an investigation would uncover nothing crooked.''

"The gyps,'' Corrigan said, then stopped at Beaucamp's glare. "I mean, the guaranteed income people, or welfares as we called them when I was a kid, well, the GIP whites will be screaming discrimination.''

"The whites could have volunteered,'' the President said.

Beaucamp's lip was curled. "Somebody spread the word. Of course, that would have nothing to do with lack of Caucasian applications.''

Kingbrook rumbled like a volcano preparing to erupt. He said, "What're we arguing about this for? This . . . Bird City . . . was built over an all-colored section. So why shouldn't its citizens be colored? Let's stick to the point. You want to build more cities just like this, Mr. President, extend them outwards from this until you have one solid megalopolis on stilts extending from Santa Barbara to Long Beach. But you can't build here or in other states without absolutely bankrupting the country. So you want to get us to back your legislative proposals for your so-called ORE. That is, split the economy of the nation in half. One half will continue operating just as before; that half will be made up of private-enterprise industries and of the taxpayers who own or work for these industries. This half will continue to buy and sell and use money as it has always done.

"But the other half will be composed of GIP's, living in cities like this, and the government will take care of their every need. The government will do this by automating the mines, farms, and industries it now owns or plans on obtaining. It will not use money anywhere in its operations, and the entire process of input-output will be a closed circuit. Everybody in ORE will be GIP personnel, even the federal and state government service, except, of course, that the federal, legislative, and executive branches will maintain their proper jurisdiction."

"That *sounds* great," Corrigan said. "The ultimate result, or so you've *said*, Mr. President, is to relieve the taxpayer of his crushing burden and to give the GIP a position in society in which he will no longer be considered by others as a parasite. It sounds appealing. But there are many of us who aren't fooled by your fine talk."

"I'm not trying to fool anybody," the President said.

Corrigan said, angrily, "It's obvious what the end result will be! When the taxpayer sees the GIP living like a king without turning a hand while he has to work his tail off, he's going to want the same deal. And those who refuse to give up won't have enough money to back their stand because the GIP won't be spending any money. The small businessmen who live off their sales to the GIP will go under. And the larger businesses will, too. Eventually, the businessman and his employees will fold their fiscal and pecuniary tents and go to live in your everything-free cornucopias!

"So, if we're seduced by your beautiful scheme for a half-and-half economy, we'll take the first step into the quicksand. After that, it'll be too late to back out. Down we go!"

"I'd say, *Up we go*," the President said. "So! It's All-or-None, as far as you're concerned? And you vote for None! Well, gentlemen, over one-half of the nation is saying All because that's the only way to go and they've nothing to lose and everything to gain. If you kill the switchover legislation in Congress, I'll see that the issues are submitted to the people for their yea or nay. But that would take too much time, and time is vital. Time is what I'm buying. Or I should say, trading."

Beaucamp said, "Mr. President, you didn't point out the racial composition of the city just to pass the time."

The President began pacing back and forth before them. He said, "The civil rights revolution was born about the same time that you and I, Mr. Beaucamp, were born. Yet, it's still far from achieving its goals. In some aspects, it's regressed. It was tragic that the Negroes began to get the education and political power they needed for advancement just as automation began to bloom. The Negro found that there were only jobs for the professionals and the skilled. The unskilled were shut out. This happened to the untrained white, too, and competition for work between the unskilled white and black became bitter. Bloodily bitter, as the past few years have shown us."

"We know what's been going on, Mr. President," Beaucamp said.

"Yes. Well, it's true isn't it, that the black as a rule, doesn't particularly care to associate or live with the whites? He just wants the same things whites have. But at the present rate of progress, it'll take a hundred years or more before he gets them. In fact, he may never do so if the present economy continues."

Kingbrook rumbled, "The point, Mr. President!"

The President stopped pacing. He looked hard at them and said, "But in an economy of abundance, in this type of city, he—the Negro—will have everything the whites have. He will have a high standard of living, a true democracy, color-free justice. He'll have his own judges, police, legislators. If he doesn't care to, he doesn't ever have to have any personal contact with whites."

Kingbrook's cigar sagged. Beaucamp sucked in his breath. Corrigan jumped up from his chair.

Beaucamp said, "That's ghettoism!"

"Not in the original sense," the President said. "The truth now, Mr. Beaucamp. Don't your people prefer to live with their own kind? Where they'll be free of that shadow, that wall, always between white and colored in this country?"

Beaucamp said, "Not to have to put up with honkeys! Excuse the expression, sir. It slipped out. You know we would! But . . ."

"No one will be forbidden to live in any community he chooses. There won't be any discrimination on the federal level. Those in the government, military, or Nature rehabilitation service will have equal opportunity. But, given the choice . . ."

The President turned to Kingbrook and Corrigan. "Publicly, you two have always stood for integration. You would have committed political suicide, otherwise. But I know your private opinions. You have also been strong states-righters. No secret about that. So, when the economy of abundance is in full swing, the states will become self-sufficient. They won't depend on federal funds."

"Because there'll be no dependence on money?" Corrigan said. "Because there'll be no money? Because money will be as extinct as the dodo?"

The ridges on Kingbrook's face shifted as if they were

the gray backs of an elephant herd milling around to catch a strange scent. He said, "I'm not blasphemous. But now I think I know how Christ felt when tempted by Satan."

He stopped, realizing that he had made a Freudian slip.

"And you're not Christ and I'm not Satan," he said hurriedly. "We're just human beings trying to find a mutually agreeable way out of this mess."

Beaucamp said, "We're horse traders. And the horse is the future. A dream. Or a nightmare."

The President looked at his watch and said, "What about it, Mr. Beaucamp?"

"What can I trade? A dream of an end to contempt, dislike, hatred, treachery, oppression. A dream of the shadow gone, the wall down. Now you offer me abundance, dignity, and joy—if my people stay within the plastic walls."

"I don't know what will develop after the walls of the cities have been built," the President said. "But there is nothing evil about self-segregation, if it's not compulsive. It's done all the time by human beings of every type. If it weren't, you wouldn't have social classes, clubs, etc. And if, after our citizens are given the best in housing and food, luxuries, a free lifelong education, a wide spectrum of recreations, everything within reason, if they still go to Hell, then we might as well give up on the species."

"A man needs incentive; he needs work. By the sweat of his brow . . ." Kingbrook said.

Kingbrook was too old, the President thought. He was half-stone, and the stone thought stone thoughts and spoke stone words. The President looked out the big window. Perhaps it had been a mistake to build such a "futuristic" city. It would be difficult enough for the new citizens to adjust. Perhaps the dome of Bird City should have contained buildings resembling those they now lived in. Later, more radical structures could have been introduced.

As it was, the ovoid shape was supposed to give a sense of security, a feeling of return-to-the-womb and also to suggest a rebirth. Just now, they looked like so many space capsules ready to take off into the blue the moment the button was pressed.

But this city, and those that would be added to it, meant a sharp break with the past, and any break always caused some pain.

He turned when someone coughed behind him. Senator Kingbrook was standing, his hand on his chest. The senator was going to make a speech.

The President looked at his watch and shook his head. Kingbrook smiled as if the smile hurt him, and he dropped his hand.

"It's yes, Mr. President. I'll back you all the way. And the impeachment proceedings will be dropped, of course. But . . ."

"I don't want to be rude, " the President said. "But you can save your justifications for your constituents."

Beaucamp said, "I say yes. Only . . ."

"No ifs, ands, or buts."

"No. Only . . ."

"And you, Governor Corrigan?" the President said.

Corrigan said, "All of us are going along with you for reasons that shouldn't be considered—from the viewpoint of ideals. But then, who really ever has? I say yes. But . . ."

"No speeches, please," the President said. He smiled slightly. "Unless I make them. Your motives don't really matter, gentlemen, as long as your decisions are for the good of the American public. Which they are. And for the good of the world, too, because all other nations are going to follow our example. As I said, this means the death of capitalism, but it also means the death of socialism and communism, too.''

He looked at his watch again. ''I thank you, gentlemen.''

They looked as if they would like to continue talking, but they left. There was a delay of a few seconds before the next group entered.

He felt weary, even though he knew that he would win out. The years ahead would be times of trouble, of crises, of pain and agony, of successes and failures. At least, mankind would no longer be drifting towards anarchy. Man would be deliberately shaping—reshaping—his society, turning topsyturvy an ancient and obsolete economy, good enough in its time but no longer applicable. At the same time, he would be tearing down the old cities and restoring Nature to something of its pristine condition, healing savage wounds inflicted by senseless selfish men in the past, cleansing the air, the poisoned rivers and lakes, growing new forests, permitting the wild creatures to flourish in their redeemed land. Man, the greedy savage child, had stripped the earth, killed the wild, fouled his own nest.

His anger, he suddenly realized, had been to divert him from that other feeling. Somehow, he had betrayed an ideal. He could not define the betrayal, because he knew that he was doing what had to be done and that that way was the only way. But he, and Kingbrook, Corrigan, and Beaucamp, had also felt this. He had seen it on their faces, like ectoplasm escaping the grasp of their minds.

A man had to be realistic. To gain one thing, you had to give up another. Life—the universe—was give and take, input and output, energy surrendered to conquer energy.

In short, politics. Compromises.

The door slid into the recess in the walls. Five men single-filed in. The President weighed each in the balance, anticipating his arguments and visualizing the bait which he would grab even if he saw the hook.

He said, "Gentlemen, be seated if you wish."

He looked at his watch and began to talk.

Riders of the Purple Wage

or
The Great Gavage

If Jules Verne could really have looked into the future, say 1966 A.D., he would have crapped in his pants. And 2166, oh, my!

—from Grandpa Winnegan's unpublished Ms., *How I Screwed Uncle Sam & Other Private Ejaculations*

THE COCK THAT CROWED BACKWARDS

Un and Sub, the giants, are grinding him for bread.

Broken pieces float up through the wine of sleep. Vast treadings crush abysmal grapes for the incubus sacrament.

He as Simple Simon fishes in his soul as pail for the leviathan.

He groans, half-wakes, turns over, sweating dark oceans, and groans again. Un and Sub, putting their backs to their work, turn the stone wheels of the sunken mill, muttering Fie, fye, fo, fum. Eyes glittering orange-red as a cat's in a cubbyhole, teeth dull white digits in the murky arithmetic.

Un and Sub, Simple Simons themselves, busily mix metaphors non-self-consciously.

Dunghill and cock's egg: up rises the cockatrice and gives first crow, two more to come, in the flushrush of blood of dawn of I-am-the-erection-and-the-strife.

It grows out and out until weight and length merge to curve it over, a not-yet weeping willow or broken reed. The one-eyed red head peeks over the edge of bed. It rests its chinless jaw, then, as body swells, slides over and down. Looking monocularly this way and those, it sniffs archaically across the floor and heads for the door, left open by the lapsus linguae of malingering sentinels.

A loud braying from the center of the room makes it turn back. The three-legged ass, Baalim's easel, is hee-hawing. On the easel is the "canvas," an oval shallow pan of irradiated plastic, specially treated. The canvas is two meters high and forty-four centimeters deep. Within the painting is a scene that must be finished by tomorrow.

. As much sculpture as painting, the figures are in alto-relief, rounded, some nearer the back of the pan than others. They glow with light from outside and also from the self-luminous plastic of the "canvas." The light seems to enter the figures, soak awhile, then break loose. The light is pale red, the red of dawn, of blood watered with tears, of anger, of ink on the debit side of the ledger.

This is one of his Dog Series: *Dogmas from a Dog, The Aerial Dogfight, Dog Days, The Sundog, Dog Reversed, The Dog of Flinders, Dog Berries, Dog Catcher,*

Lying Doggo, The Dog of the Right Angle and *Improvisations on a Dog.*

Socrates, Ben Jonson, Cellini, Swedenborg, Li Po, and Hiawatha are roistering in the Mermaid Tavern. Through a window, Daedalus is seen on top of the battlements of Cnossus, shoving a rocket up the ass of his son, Icarus, to give him a jet-assisted takeoff for his famous flight. In one corner crouches Og, Son of Fire. He gnaws on a sabertooth bone and paints bison and mammoths on the mildewed plaster. The barmaid, Athena, is bending over the table where she is serving nectar and pretzels to her distinguished customers. Aristotle, wearing goat's horns, is behind her. He has lifted her skirt and is tupping her from behind. The ashes from the cigarette dangling from his smirking lips have fallen onto her skirt, which is beginning to smoke. In the doorway of the men's room, a drunken Batman succumbs to a long-pressed desire and attempts to bugger the Boy Wonder. Through another window is a lake on the surface of which a man is walking, a green-tarnished halo hovering over his head. Behind him a periscope sticks out of the water.

Prehensile, the penisnake wraps itself around the brush and begins to pain. The brush is a small cylinder attached at one end to a hose which runs to a dome-shaped machine. From the other end of the cylinder extends a nozzle. The aperture of this can be decreased or increased by rotation of a thumb-dial on the cylinder. The paint which the nozzle deposits in a fine spray or in a thick stream or in whatever color or hue desired is controlled by several dials on the cylinder.

Furiously, proboscisean, it builds up another figure layer by layer. Then, it sniffs a musty odor of must and drops the brush and slides out the door and down the bend of wall of oval hall, describing the scrawl of legless creatures, a writing in the sand which all may read but few understand. Blood pumppumps in rhythm with the mills of Un and Sub to feed and swill the hot-blooded reptile. But the walls, detecting intrusive mass and extrusive desire, glow.

He groans, and the glandular cobra rises and sways to the fluting of his wish for cuntcealment. Let there not be light! The lights must be his cloaka. Speed past mother's room, nearest the exit. Ah! Sighs softly in relief but air whistles through the vertical and tight mouth, announcing the departure of the exsupress for Desideratum.

The door has become archaic; it has a keyhole. Quick! Up the ramp and out of the house through the keyhole and out onto the street. One person abroad a broad, a young woman with phosphorescent silver hair and snatch to match.

Out and down the street and coiling around her ankle. She looks down with surprise and then fear. He likes this; too willing were too many. He's found a diamond in the ruff.

Up around her kitten-ear-soft leg, around and around, and sliding across the dale of groin. Nuzzling the tender corkscrewed hairs and then, self-Tantalus, detouring up the slight convex of belly, saying hello to the bellybutton, pressing on it to ring upstairs, around and around the narrow waist and shyly and quickly snatching a kiss from each nipple. Then back down to form an expedition for climbing the mons veneris and planting the flag thereon.

Oh, delectation tabu and sickersacrosanct! There's a baby in there, ectoplasm beginning to form in eager preanticipation of actuality. Drop, egg, and shoot the chuty-chutes of flesh, hastening to gulp the lucky Micromoby Dick, outwriggling its million million brothers, survival of the fightingest.

A vast croaking fills the hall. The hot breath chills the skin. He sweats. Icicles coat the tumorous fuselage, and it sags under the weight of ice, and fog rolls around, whistling past the struts, and the ailerons and elevators are locked in ice, and he's losing altitude fast. Get up, get up! Venusberg somewhere ahead in the mists; Tannhäuser, blow your strumpets, send up your flares, I'm in a nosedive.

Mother's door has opened. A toad squatfills the ovoid doorway. Its dewlap rises and falls bellows-like; its toothless mouth gawps. Ginungagap. Forked tongue shoots out and curls around the boar cunstrictor. He cries out with both mouths and jerks this way and those. The waves of denial run through. Two webbed paws bend and tie the flopping body into a knot—a runny shapeshank, of course.

The woman strolls on. Wait for me! Out the flood roars, crashes into the knot, roars back, ebb clashing with flood. Too much and only one way to go. He jerkspurts, the firmament of waters falling, no Noah's ark or arc; he novas, a shatter of millions of glowing wriggling meteors, flashes in the pan of existence.

Thigh kingdom come. Groin and belly encased in musty armor, and he cold, wet, and trembling.

GOD'S PATENT ON DAWN EXPIRES

. . . the following spoken by Alfred Melophon Voxpopper, of the Aurora Pushups and Coffee Hour, Channel 69B. Lines taped during the 50th Folk Art Center Annual Demonstration and Competition, Beverly Hills, level 14. Spoken by Omar Bacchylides Runic, extemporaneously if you discount some forethought during the previous evening at the nonpublic tavern, The Private Universe, and you may because Runic did not remember a thing about that evening. Despite which he won First

Philip José Farmer

Laurel Wreath A, there being no Second, Third, etc.,
wreaths classified as A through Z, God bless our democracy.

A gray-pink salmon leaping up the falls of night
Into the spawning pool of another day.

Dawn—the red roar of the heliac bull
Charging over the horizon.

The photonic blood of bleeding night,
Stabbed by the assassin sun.

and so on for fifty lines punctuated and fractured by
cheers, handclaps, boos, hisses, and yelps.

Chib is half-awake. He peeps down into the narrowing
dark as the dream roars off into the subway tunnel. He
peeps through barely opened lids at the other reality:
consciousness.

"Let my peeper go!" he groans with Moses and so,
thinking of long beards and horns (courtesy of Michelangelo), he thinks of his great-great-grandfather.

The will, a crowbar, forces his eyelids open. He sees
the fido which spans the wall opposite him and curves
up over half the ceiling. Dawn, the paladin of the sun,
is flinging its gray gauntlet down.

Channel 69B, YOUR FAVORITE CHANNEL, LA's
own, brings you dawn. (Deception in depth. Nature's
false dawn shadowed forth with electrons shaped by devices shaped by man.)

Wake up with the sun in your heart and a song on your
lips! Thrill to the stirring lines of Omar Runic! See dawn
as the birds in the trees, as God, see it!

Voxpopper chants the lines softly while Grieg's *Anitra*
wells softly. The old Norwegian never dreamed of this
audience and just as well. A young man, Chibiabos El-

greco Winnegan, has a sticky wick, courtesy of a late gusher in the oilfield of the unconscious.

"Off your ass and onto your steed," Chib says. "Pegasus runs today."

He speaks, thinks, lives in the present tensely.

Chib climbs out of bed and shoves it into the wall. To leave the bed sticking out, rumpled as an old drunkard's tongue, would fracture the aesthetics of his room, destroy that curve that is the reflection of the basic universe, and hinder him in his work.

The room is a huge ovoid and in a corner is a small ovoid, the toilet and shower. He comes out of it looking like one of Homer's god-like Achaeans, massively thighed, great-armed, golden-brown-skinned, blue-eyed, auburn-haired—although beardless. The phone is simulating the tocsin of a South American tree frog he once heard over Channel 122.

"Open O sesame!"

INTER CAECOS REGNAT LUSCUS

The face of Rex Luscus spreads across the fido, the pores of skin like the cratered fields of a World War I battlefield. He wears a black monocle over the left eye, ripped out in a brawl among art critics during the *I Love Rembrandt Lecture Series,* Channel 109. Although he has enough pull to get a priority for eye-replacement, he has refused.

"Inter caecos regnat luscus," he says when asked about it and quite often when not. "Translation: among the blind, the one-eyed man is king. That's why I renamed myself Rex Luscus, that is, King One-eyed."

There is a rumor, fostered by Luscus, that he will

permit the bioboys to put in an artificial protein eye when he sees the works of an artist great enough to justify focal vision. It is also rumored that he may do so soon, because of his discovery of Chibiabos Elgreco Winnegan.

Luscus looks hungrily (he swears by adverbs) at Chib's tomentum and outlying regions. Chib swells, not with tumescence but with anger.

Luscus says, smoothly, "Honey, I just want to reassure myself that you're up and about the tremendously important business of this day. You must be ready for the showing, must! But now I see you, I'm reminded I've not eaten yet. What about breakfast with me?"

"What're we eating?" Chib says. He does not wait for a reply. "No. I've too much to do today. Close O sesame!"

Rex Luscus' face fades away, goatlike, or, as he prefers to describe it, the face of Pan, a Faunus of the arts. He has even had his ears trimmed to a point. Real cute.

"Baa-aa-aa!" Chib bleats at the phantom. "Ba! Humbuggery! I'll never kiss your ass, Luscus, or let you kiss mine. Even if I lose the grant!"

The phone bells again. The dark face of Rousseau Red Hawk appears. His nose is as the eagle's, and his eyes are broken black glass. His broad forehead is bound with a strip of red cloth, which circles the straight black hair that glides down to his shoulders. His shirt is buckskin; a necklace of beads hangs from his neck. He looks like a Plains Indian, although Sitting Bull, Crazy Horse, or the noblest Roman Nose of them all would have kicked him out of the tribe. Not that they were anti-Semitic, they just could not have respected a brave who broke out into hives when near a horse.

Born Julius Applebaum, he legally became Rousseau Red Hawk on his Naming Day. Just returned from the forest reprimevalized, he is now reveling in the accursed fleshpots of a decadent civilization.

"How're you, Chib? The gang's wondering how soon you'll get here?"

"Join you? I haven't had breakfast yet, and I've a thousand things to do to get ready for the showing. I'll see you at noon!"

"You missed out on the fun last night. Some goddam Egyptians tried to feel the girls up, but we salaamed them against the walls."

Rousseau vanished like the last of the red men.

Chib thinks of breakfast just as the intercom whistles. Open O sesame! He sees the living room. Smoke, too thick and furious for the air-conditioning to whisk away, roils. At the far end of the ovoid, his little half-brother and half-sister sleep on a flato. Playing Mama-and-friend, they fell asleep, their mouths open in blessed innocence, beautiful as only sleeping children can be. Opposite the closed eyes of each is an unwinking eye like that of a Mongolian Cyclops.

"Ain't's they cute?" Mama says. "The darlings were just too tired to toddle off."

The table is round. The aged knights and ladies are gathered around it for the latest quest of the ace, king, queen, and jack. They are armored only in layer upon layer of fat. Mama's jowls hang down like banners on a windless day. Her breasts creep and quiver on the table, bulge, and ripple.

"A gam of gamblers," he says aloud, looking at the fat faces, the tremendous tits, the rampant rumps. They raise their eyebrows. What the hell's the mad genius talking about now?

"Is your kid really retarded?" says one of Mama's friends, and they laugh and drink some more beer. Angela Ninon, not wanting to miss out on this deal and figuring Mama will soon turn on the sprayers anyway, pisses down her leg. They laugh at this, and William Conqueror says, "I open."

"I'm always open," Mama says, and they shriek with laughter.

Chib would like to cry. He does not cry, although he has been encouraged from childhood to cry any time he feels like it.

—It makes you feel better and look at the Vikings, what men they were and they cried like babies whenever they felt like it—

Courtesy of Channel 202 on the popular program *What's A Mother Done?*

He does not cry because he feels like a man who thinks about the mother he loved and who is dead but who died a long time ago. His mother has been long buried under a landslide of flesh. When he was sixteen, he had had a lovely mother.

Then she cut him off.

THE FAMILY THAT BLOWS
IS THE FAMILY THAT GROWS

—from a poem by Edgar A. Grist, via Channel 88

"Son, I don't get much out of this. I just do it because I love you."

Then, fat, fat, fat! Where did she go? Down into the adipose abyss. Disappearing as she grew larger.

"Sonny, you could at least wrestle with me a little now and then."

"You cut me off, Mama. That was all right. I'm a big boy now. But you haven't any right to expect me to want to take it up again."

"You don't love me any more!"

"What's for breakfast, Mama?" Chib says.

"I'm holding a good hand, Chibby," Mama says. "As you've told me so many times, you're a big boy. Just this once, get your own breakfast."

"What'd you call me for?"

"I forgot when your exhibition starts. I wanted to get some sleep before I went."

"14:30, Mama, but you don't have to go."

Rouged green lips part like a gangrened wound. She scratches one rouged nipple. "Oh, I want to be there. I don't want to miss my own son's artistic triumphs. Do you think you'll get the grant?"

"If I don't, it's Egypt for us," he says.

"Those stinking Arabs!" says William Conqueror.

"It's the Bureau that's doing it, not the Arabs," Chib says. "The Arabs moved for the same reason we may have to move."

From Grandpa's unpublished Ms.:

> Who ever would have thought that Beverly Hills would become anti-Semitic?

"I don't want to go to Egypt!" Mama wails. "You got to get that grant, Chibby. I don't want to leave the clutch. I was born and raised here, well, on the tenth level, anyway, and when I moved all my friends went along. I won't go!"

"Don't cry, Mama," Chib says, feeling distress despite himself. "Don't cry. The government can't force you to go, you know. You got your rights."

"If you want to keep on having goodies, you'll go," says Conqueror. "Unless Chib wins the grant, that is. And I wouldn't blame him if he didn't even try to win it. It ain't his fault you can't say no to Uncle Sam. You got your purple and the yap Chib makes from selling his paintings. Yet it ain't enough. You spend faster than you get it."

Mama screams with fury at William, and they're off. Chib cuts off fido. Hell with breakfast; he'll eat later. His final painting for the Festival must be finished by noon. He presses a plate, and the bare egg-shaped room opens here and there, and painting equipment comes out like a gift from the electronic gods. Zeuxis would flip and Van Gogh would get the shakes if they could see the canvas and palette and brush Chib uses.

The process of painting involves the individual bending and twisting of thousands of wires into different shapes at various depths. The wires are so thin they can be seen only with magnifiers and manipulated with exceedingly delicate pliers. Hence, the goggles he wears and the long almost-gossamer instrument in his hand when he is in the first stages of creating a painting. After hundreds of hours of slow and patient labor (of love), the wires are arranged.

Chib removes his goggles to perceive the overall effect. He then uses the paint-sprayer to cover the wires with the colors and hues he desires. The paint dries hard within a few minutes. Chib attaches electrical leads to the pan and presses a button to deliver a tiny voltage through the wires. These glow beneath the paint and, Lilliputian fuses, disappear in blue smoke.

The result is a three-dimensional work composed of hard shells of paint on several levels below the exterior shell. The shells are of varying thicknesses and all are so thin that light slips through the upper to the inner shell when the painting is turned at angles. Parts of the shells are simply reflectors to intensify the light so that the inner images may be more visible.

When being shown, the painting is on a self-moving pedestal which turns the painting 12 degrees to the left from the center.

The fido tocsins. Chib, cursing, thinks of disconnecting it. At least, it's not the intercom with his mother calling hysterically. Not yet, anyway. She'll call soon enough if she loses heavily at poker.

Open O sesame!

SING, O MEWS, OF UNCLE SAM

Grandpa writes in his *Private Ejaculations*:

> Twenty-five years after I fled with twenty billion dollars and then supposedly died of a heart attack, Falco Accipiter is on my trail again. The IRB detective who named himself Falcon Hawk when he entered his profession. What an egotist! Yet, he is as sharp-eyed and relentless as a bird of prey, and I would shiver if I were not too old to be frightened by mere human beings. Who loosed the jesses and hood? How did he pick up the old and cold scent?

Accipiter's face is that of an overly suspicious peregrine that tries to look everywhere while it soars, that peers up its own anus to make sure that no duck has taken refuge there. The pale blue eyes fling glances like knives shot out of a shirtsleeve and hurled with a twist of the wrist. They scan all with sherlockian intake of minute and significant detail. His head turns back and forth, ears twitching, nostrils expanding and collapsing, all radar and sonar and odar.

"Mr. Winnegan, I'm sorry to call so early. Did I get you out of bed?"

"It's obvious you didn't!" Chib says. "Don't bother to introduce yourself. I know you. You've been shadowing me for three days."

Accipiter does not redden. Master of control, he does all his blushing in the depths of his bowels, where no one can see. "If you know me, perhaps you can tell me why I'm calling you?"

"Would I be dumbshit enough to tell you?"

"Mr. Winnegan, I'd like to talk to you about your great-great-grandfather."

"He's been dead for twenty-five years!" Chib cries. "Forget him. And don't bother me. Don't try for a search warrant. No judge would give you one. A man's home is his hassle . . . I mean castle."

He thinks of Mama and what the day is going to be like unless he gets out soon. But he has to finish the painting.

"Fade off, Accipiter," Chib says. "I think I'll report you to the BPHR. I'm sure you got a fido inside that silly-looking hat of yours."

Accipiter's face is as smooth and unmoving as an alabaster carving of the falcon-god Horus. He may have a little gas bulging his intestines. If so, he slips it out unnoticed.

"Very well, Mr. Winnegan. But you're not getting rid of me that easily. After all . . ."

"Fade out!"

The intercom whistles thrice. What I tell you three times is Grandpa. "I was eavesdropping," says the 120-year-old voice, hollow and deep as an echo from a Pharaoh's tomb. "I want to see you before you leave. That is, if you can spare the Ancient of Daze a few minutes."

"Always, Grandpa," Chib says, thinking of how much he loves the old man. "You need any food?"

"Yes, and for the mind, too."

Der Tag. Dies Irae. Götterdämmerung. Armageddon. Things are closing in. Make-or-break day. Go-no-go time. All these calls and a feeling of more to come. What will the end of the day bring?

THE TROCHE SUN SLIPS INTO
THE SORE THROAT OF NIGHT

—from Omar Runic

Chib walks toward the convex door, which rolls into the interstices between the walls. The focus of the house is the oval family room. In the first quadrant, going clockwise, is the kitchen, separated from the family room by six-meter-high accordion screens, painted with scenes from Egyptian tombs by Chib, his too subtle comment on modern food. Seven slim pillars around the family room mark the borders of room and corridor. Between the pillars are more tall accordion screens, painted by Chib during his Amerind mythology phase.

The corridor is also oval-shaped; every room in the house opens onto it. There are seven rooms, six bedroom-workroom-study-toilet-shower combinations. The seventh is a storeroom.

Little eggs within bigger eggs within great eggs within a megamonolith on a planetary pear within an ovoid universe, the latest cosmogony indicating that infinity has the form of a hen's fruit. God broods over the abyss and cackles every trillion years or so.

Chib cuts across the hall, passes between two pillars, carved by him into nymphet caryatids, and enters the family room. His mother looks sidewise at her son, who she thinks is rapidly approaching insanity if he has not already overshot his mark. It's partly her fault; she shouldn't have gotten disgusted and in a moment of wackiness called It off. Now, she's fat and ugly, oh, God, so fat and ugly. She can't reasonably or even unreasonably hope to start up again.

It's only natural, she keeps telling herself, sighing, resentful, teary, that he's abandoned the love of his mother for the strange, firm, shapely delights of young women. But to give them up, too? He's not a bisex. He quit all that when he was thirteen. So what's the reason for his chastity? He isn't in love with the fornixator, either, which she would understand, even if she did not approve.

Oh, God, where did I go wrong? And then, There's nothing wrong with me. He's going crazy like his father—Raleigh Renaissance, I think his name was—and his aunt and his great-great-grandfather. It's all that painting and those radicals, the Young Radishes, he runs around with. He's too artistic, too sensitive. Oh, God, if something happens to my little boy, I'll have to go to Egypt.

Chib knows her thoughts since she's voiced them so many times and is not capable of having new ones. He passes the round table without a word. The knights and ladies of the canned Camelot see him through a beery veil.

In the kitchen, he opens an oval door in the wall. He removes a tray with food in covered dishes and cups, all wrapped in plastic.

"Aren't you going to eat with us?"

"Don't whine, Mama," he says and goes back to his room to pick up some cigars for his Grandpa. The door, detecting, amplifying, and transmitting the shifting but recognizable eidolon of epidermal electrical fields to the activating mechanism, balks. Chib is too upset. Magnetic maelstroms rage over his skin and distort the spectral configuration. The door half-rolls out, rolls in, changes its minds again, rolls out, rolls in.

Chib kicks the door and it becomes completely blocked. He decides he'll have a video or vocal sesame put in. Trouble is, he's short of units and coupons and can't buy the materials. He shrugs and walks along the curving, one-walled hall and stops in front of Grandpa's door, hidden from view of those in the living room by the kitchen screens.

> "For he sang of peace and freedom,
> Sang of beauty, love, and longing;
> Sang of death, and life undying
> In the Islands of the Blessed,
> In the kingdom of Ponemah,
> In the land of the Hereafter.
> Very dear to Hiawatha
> Was the gentle Chibiabos."

Chib chants the passwords; the door rolls back.

Light glares out, a yellowish red-tinged light that is Grandpa's own creation. Looking into the convex oval door is like looking into the lens of a madman's eyeball. Grandpa, in the middle of the room, has a white beard falling to midthigh and white hair cataracting to just below the back of his knees. Although beard and headhair conceal his nakedness, and he is not out in public, he wears a pair of shorts. Grandpa is somewhat old-fashioned, forgivable in a man of twelve decadencies.

Like Rex Luscus, he is one-eyed. He smiles with his own teeth, grown from buds transplanted thirty years ago. A big green cigar sticks out of one corner of his full red mouth. His nose is broad and smeared as if time had stepped upon it with a heavy foot. His forehead and cheeks are broad, perhaps due to a shot of Ojibway blood in his veins, though he was born Finnegan and even sweats celtically, giving off an aroma of whiskey. He holds his head high, and the blue-gray eye is like a pool at the bottom of a prediluvian pothole, remnant of a melted glacier.

All in all, Grandpa's face is Odin's as he returns from the Well of Mimir, wondering if he paid too great a price. Or it is the face of the windbeaten, sandblown Sphinx of Gizeh.

"Forty centuries of hysteria look down upon you, to paraphrase Napoleon," Grandpa says. "The rockhead of the ages. *What, then is Man?* sayeth the New Sphinx, Oedipus having resolved the question of the Old Sphinx and settling nothing because She had already delivered another of her kind, a smartass kid with a question nobody's been able to answer yet. And perhaps just as well it can't be."

"You talk funny," Chib says. "But I like it."

He grins at Grandpa, loving him.

"You sneak into here every day, not so much from love for me as to gain knowledge and insight. I have seen all, heard everything, and thought more than a little. I voyaged much before I took refuge in this room a quarter of a century ago. Yet confinement here has been the greatest Odyssey of all.

THE ANCIENT MARINATOR

I call myself. A marinade of wisdom steeped in the brine of over-salted cynicism and too long a life."

"You smile so, you must have just had a woman," Chib teases.

"No, my boy. I lost the tension in my ramrod thirty years ago. And I thank God for that, since it removes from me the temptation of fornication, not to mention masturbation. However, I have other energies left, hence, scope for other sins, and these are even more serious.

"Aside from the sin of sexual commission, which paradoxically involves the sin of sexual emission, I had other reasons for not asking that Old Black Magician Science for shots to starch me out again. I was too old for young girls to be attracted to me for anything but money. And I was too much a poet, a lover of beauty, to take on the wrinkled blisters of my generation or several just before mine.

"So now you see, my son. My clapper swings limberly in the bell of my sex. Ding, dong, ding, dong. A lot of dong, but not much ding."

Grandpa laughs deeply, a lion's roar with a spray of doves.

"I am but the mouthpiece of the ancients, a shyster pleading for long-dead clients. Come not to bury but to praise and forced by my sense of fairness to admit the faults of the past, too. I'm a queer crabbed old man, pent like Merlin in his tree trunk. Samolxis, the Thracian bear god, hibernating in his cave. The Last of the Seven Sleepers."

Grandpa goes to the slender plastic tube depending from the ceiling and pulls down the folding handles of the eyepiece.

"Accipiter is hovering outside our house. He smells something rotten in Beverly Hills, level 14. Could it be that Win-again Winnegan isn't dead? Uncle Sam is like a diplodocus kicked in the ass. It takes twenty-five years for the message to reach its brain."

Tears appear in Chib's eyes. He says, "Oh, God, Grandpa, I don't want anything to happen to you."

"What can happen to a 120-year-old man besides failure of brain or kidneys?"

"With all due respect, Grandpa," Chib says, "you do rattle on."

"Call me Id's mill," Grandpa says. "The flour it yields is baked in the strange oven of my ego—or half-baked, if you please."

Chib grins through his tears and says, "They taught me at school that puns are cheap and vulgar."

"What's good enough for Homer, Aristophanes, Rabelais, and Shakespeare is good enough for me. By the way, speaking of cheap and vulgar, I met your mother in the hall last night, before the poker party started. I was just leaving the kitchen with a bottle of booze. She almost fainted. But she recovered fast and pretended not to see me. Maybe she did think she'd seen a ghost. I doubt it. She'd have been blabbing all over town about it."

"She may have told her doctor," Chib says. "She saw you several weeks ago, remember? She may have mentioned it while she was bitching about her so-called dizzy spells and hallucinations."

"And the old sawbones, knowing the family history, called the IRB. Maybe."

Chib looks through the periscope's eyepiece. He rotates it and turns the knobs on the handle-ends to raise and lower the cyclops on the end of the tube outside. Accipiter is stalking around the aggregate of seven eggs, each on the end of a broad thin curved branchlike walk projecting from the central pedestal. Accipiter goes up the steps of a branch to the door of Mrs. Applebaum's. The door opens.

"He must have caught her away from the fornixator," Chib says. "And she must be lonely; she's not talking to him over fido. My God, she's fatter than Mama!"

"Why not?" Grandpa says. "Mr. and Mrs. Everyman

sit on their asses all day, drink, eat, and watch fido, and their brains run to mud and their bodies to sludge. Caesar would have had no trouble surrounding himself with fat friends these days. You ate, too, Brutus?''

Grandpa's comment, however, should not apply to Mrs. Applebaum. She has a hole in her head, and people addicted to fornixation seldom get fat. They sit or lie all day and part of the night, the needle in the fornix area of the brain delivering a series of minute electrical jolts. Indescribable ecstasy floods through their bodies with every impulse, a delight far surpassing any of food, drink, or sex. It's illegal, but the government never bothers a user unless it wants to get him for something else, since a fornic rarely has children. Twenty per cent of LA have had holes drilled in their heads and tiny shafts inserted for access of the needle. Five per cent are addicted; they waste away, seldom eating, their distended bladders spilling poisons into the bloodstream.

Chib says, ''My brother and sister must have seen you sometimes when you were sneaking out to mass. Could they . . . ?''

''They think I'm a ghost, too. In this day and age! Still, maybe it's a good sign that they can believe in something, even a spook.''

''You better stop sneaking out to Church.''

''The Church, and you, are the only things that keep me going. It was a sad day, though, when you told me you couldn't believe. You would have made a good priest—with faults, of course—and I could have had private mass and confession in this room.''

Chib says nothing. He's gone to instruction and observed services just to please Grandpa. The Church was an egg-shaped seashell which, held to the ear, gave only the distant roar of God receding like an ebb tide.

THERE ARE UNIVERSES
BEGGING FOR GODS

yet He hangs around this one looking for work.

—from Grandpa's Ms.

Grandpa takes over the eyepiece. He laughs. "The Internal Revenue Bureau! I thought it'd been disbanded! Who the hell has an income big enough to report on any more? Do you suppose it's still active just because of me? Could be."

He calls Chib back to the scope, directed towards the center of Beverly Hills. Chib has a lane of vision between the seven-egged clutches on the branched pedestals. He can see part of the central plaza, the giant ovoids of the city hall, the federal bureaus, the Folk Center, part of the massive spiral on which set the houses of worship, and the dora (from pandora) where those on the purple wage get their goods and those with extra income get their goodies. One end of the big artificial lake is visible; boats and canoes sail on it and people fish.

The irradiated plastic dome that enfolds the clutches of Beverly Hills is sky-blue. The electronic sun climbs towards the zenith. There are a few white genuine-looking images of clouds and even a V of geese migrating south, their honks coming down faintly. Very nice for those who have never been outside the walls of LA. But Chib spent two years in the World Nature Rehabilitation and Conservation Corps—the WNRCC—and he knows the difference. Almost, he decided to desert with Rousseau Red Hawk and join the neo-Amerinds. Then, he was going to become a forest ranger. But this might mean he'd end up shooting or arresting Red Hawk. Besides, he didn't want to become a sammer. And he wanted more than anything to paint.

"There's Rex Luscus," Chib says. "He's being interviewed outside the Folk Center. Quite a crowd."

THE PELLUCIDAR BREAKTHROUGH

Luscus' middle name should have been Upmanship. A man of great erudition, with privileged access to the Library of Greater LA computer, and of Ulyssean sneakiness, he is always scoring over his colleagues.

He it was who founded the Go-Go School of Criticism.

Primalux Ruskinson, his great competitor, did some extensive research when Luscus announced the title of his new philosophy. Ruskinson triumphantly announced that Luscus had taken the phrase from obsolete slang, current in the mid-twentieth century.

Luscus, in the fido interview next day, said that Ruskinson was a rather shallow scholar, which was to be expected.

Go-go was taken from the Hottentot language. In Hottentot, *go-go* meant to examine, that is, to keep looking until something about the object—in this case, the artist and his works—has been observed.

The critics got in line to sign up at the new school. Ruskinson thought of committing suicide, but instead accused Luscus of having blown his way up the ladder of success.

Luscus replied on fido that his personal life was his

own, and Ruskinson was in danger of being sued for violation of privacy. However, he deserved no more effort than a man striking at a mosquito.

"What the hell's a mosquito?" say millions of viewers. "Wish the bighead would talk language we could understand."

Luscus' voice fades off for a minute while the interpreters explain, having just been slipped a note from a monitor who's run off the word through the stations' encyclopedia.

Luscus rode on the novelty of the Go-Go School for two years.

Then he re-established his prestige, which had been slipping somewhat, with his philosophy of the Totipotent Man.

This was so popular that the Bureau of Cultural Development and Recreation requisitioned a daily one-hour slot for a year-and-a-half in the initial program to totipotentializing.

Grandpa Winnegan's penned comment in his *Private Ejaculations*:

What about The Totipotent Man, that apotheosis of individuality and complete psychosomatic development, the democratic Ubermensch, as recommended by Rex Luscus, the sexually one-sided? Poor old Uncle Sam! Trying to force the proteus of his citizens into a single stabilized shape so he can control them. And at the same time trying to encourage each and every to bring to flower his inherent capabilities—if any! The poor old long-legged, chin-whiskered, milk-hearted, flint-brained schizophrenic! Verily, the left hand knows not what the right hand is doing. As a matter of fact, the right hand doesn't know what the right hand is doing.

"What about the totipotent man?" Luscus replied to the chairman during the fourth session of the *Luscan Lecture Series*. "How does he conflict with the contemporary Zeitgeist? He doesn't. The totipotent man is the imperative of our times. He must come into being before the Golden World can be realized. How can you have a Utopia without utopians, a Golden World with humans of brass?"

It was during this Memorable Day that Luscus gave his talk on The Pellucidar Breakthrough and thereby made Chibiabos Winnegan famous. And more than incidentally gave Luscus his biggest score over his competitors.

"Pellucidar? Pellucidar?" Ruskinson mutters. "Oh, God, what's Tinker Bell doing now?"

"It'll take me some time to explain why I use this phrase to describe Winnegan's stroke of genius," Luscus continues. "First, let me seem to detour.

FROM THE ARCTIC TO ILLINOIS

"Now, Confucius once said that a bear could not fart at the North Pole without causing a big wind in Chicago.

"By this he meant that all events, therefore, all men, are interconnected in an unbreakable web. What one man does, no matter how seemingly insignificant, vibrates through the strands and affects every man."

Ho Chung Ko, before his fido on the 30th level of Lhasa, Tibet, says to his wife, "That white prick has got it all wrong. Confucius didn't say that. Lenin preserve us! I'm going to call him up and give him hell.''

His wife says, ''Let's change the channel. Pai Ting Place is on now, and . . .''

Ngombe, 10th level, Nairobi: ''The critics here are a bunch of black bastards. Now you take Luscus; he could see my genius in a second. I'm going to apply for emigration in the morning.''

Wife: ''You might at least ask me if I want to go! What about the kids . . . mother . . . friends . . . dog . . . ?'' and so on into the lionless night of self-luminous Africa.

''. . . ex-president Radinoff,'' Luscus continues, ''once said that this is the 'Age of the Plugged-In Man.' Some rather vulgar remarks have been made about this, to me, insighted phrase. But Radinoff did not mean that human society is a daisy chain. He meant that the current of modern society flows through the circuit of which we are all part. This is the Age of Complete Interconnection. No wires can hang loose; otherwise we all short-circuit. Yet, it is undeniable that life without individuality is not worth living. Every man must be a *hapax legomenon* . . .''

Ruskinson jumps up from his chair and screams, ''I know that phrase! I got you this time, Luscus!''

He is so excited he falls over in a faint, symptom of a widespread hereditary defect. When he recovers, the lecture is over. He springs to the recorder to run off what he missed. But Luscus has carefully avoided defining The Pellucidar Breakthrough. He will explain it at another lecture.

Grandpa, back at the scope, whistles. ''I feel like an astronomer. The planets are in orbit around our house, the sun. There's Accipiter, the closest, Mercury, although he's not the god of thieves but their nemesis.

Next, Benedictine, your sad-sack Venus. Hard, hard, hard! The sperm would batter their heads flat against the stony ovum. You sure she's pregnant?

"Your Mama's out there, dressed fit to kill and I wish someone would. Mother Earth headed for the perigee of the gummint store to waste your substance."

Grandpa braces himself as if on a rolling deck, the blue-black veins on his legs thick as strangling vines on an ancient oak. "Brief departure from the role of Herr Doktor Sternscheissdreckschnuppe, the great astronomer, to that of der Unterseeboot Kapitan von Schooten die Fischen in der Barrel. Ach! I zee yet das tramp schteamer, Deine Mama, yawing, pitching, rolling in the seas of alcohol. Compass lost; rhumb dumb. Three sheets to the wind. Paddlewheels spinning in the air. The black gang sweating their balls off, stoking the furnaces of frustration. Propeller tangled in the nets of neurosis. And the Great White Whale a glimmer in the black depths but coming up fast, intent on broaching her bottom, too big to miss. Poor damned vessel, I weep for her. I also vomit with disgust.

"Fire one! Fire two! Baroom! Mama rolls over, a jagged hole in her hull but not the one you're thinking of. Down she goes, nose first, as befits a devoted fellationeer, her huge aft rising into the air. Blub, blub! Full fathom five!

"And so back from undersea to outer space. Your sylvan Mars, Red Hawk, has just stepped out of the tavern. And Luscus, Jupiter, the one-eyed All-Father of Art, if you'll pardon my mixing of Nordic and Latin mythologies, is surrounded by his swarm of satellites."

EXCRETION IS THE
BITTER PART OF VALOR

Luscus says to the fido interviewers. "By this I mean
that Winnegan, like every artist, great or not, produces
art that is, first, secretion, unique to himself, then excretion. Excretion in the original sense of 'sifting out.' Creative excretion or discrete excretion. I know that my
distinguished colleagues will make fun of this analogy,
so I hereby challenge them to a fido debate whenever it
can be arranged.

"The valor comes from the courage of the artist in
showing his inner products to the public. The bitter part
comes from the fact that the artist may be rejected or
misunderstood in his time. Also from the terrible war
that takes place in the artist with the disconnected or
chaotic elements, often contradictory, which he must
unite and then mold into a unique entity. Hence my 'discrete excretion' phrase."

Fido interviewer: "Are we to understand that everything is a big pile of shit but that art makes a strange
seachange, forms it into something golden and illuminating?"

"Not exactly. But you're close. I'll elaborate and ex-
pound at a later date. At present, I want to talk about
Winnegan. Now, the lesser artists give only the surface
of things; they are photographers. But the great ones give
the interiority of objects and beings. Winnegan, however, is the first to reveal more than one interiority in a
single work of art. His invention of the alto-relief mul-
tilevel technique enables him to epiphanize—show
forth—subterranean layer upon layer."

Primalux Ruskinson, loudly, "The Great Onion Peeler of Painting!"

Luscus, calmly after the laughter has died: "In one sense, that is well put. Great art, like an onion, brings tears to the eyes. However, the light on Winnegan's paintings is not just a reflection; it is sucked in, digested, and then fractured forth. Each of the broken beams makes visible, not various aspects of the figures beneath, but whole figures. Worlds, I might say.

"I call this The Pellucidar Breakthrough. Pellucidar is the hollow interior of our planet, as depicted in a now forgotten fantasy-romance of the twentieth-century writer, Edgar Rice Burroughs, creator of the immortal Tarzan."

Ruskinson moans and feels faint again. "Pellucid! Pellucidar! Luscus, you punning exhumist bastard!"

"Burroughs' hero penetrated the crust of Earth to discover another world inside. This was, in some ways, the reverse of the exterior, continents where the surface seas are, and vice versa. Just so, Winnegan has discovered an inner world, the obverse of the public image Everyman projects. And, like Burroughs' hero, he has returned with a stunning narrative of psychic dangers and exploration.

"And just as the fictional hero found his Pellucidar to be populated with stone-age men and dinosaurs, so Winnegan's world is, though absolutely modern in one sense, archaic in another. Abysmally pristine. Yet, in the illumination of Winnegan's world, there is an evil and inscrutable patch of blackness, and that is paralleled in Pellucidar by the tiny fixed moon which casts a chilling and unmoving shadow.

"Now, I did intend that the ordinary 'pellucid' should be part of Pellucidar. Yet 'pellucid' means 'reflecting light evenly from all surfaces' or 'admitting maximum passage of light without diffusion or distortion.' Winnegan's paintings do just the opposite. But—under the bro-

ken and twisted light, the acute observer can see a pri-
meval luminosity, even and straight. This is the light that
links all the fractures and multilevels, the light I was
thinking of in my earlier discussion of the 'Age of the
Plugged-In Man' and the polar bear.

"By intent scrutiny, a viewer may detect this, feel, as
it were, the photonic fremitus of the heartbeat of Winnegan's world."

Ruskinson almost faints. Luscus' smile and black
monocle make him look like a pirate who has just taken
a Spanish galleon loaded with gold.

Grandpa, still at the scope, says, "And there's Maryam bint Yusuf, the Egyptian backwoodswoman you were
telling me about. Your Saturn, aloof, regal, cold, and
wearing one of those suspended whirling manycolored
hats that're all the rage. Saturn's rings? Or a halo?"

"She's beautiful, and she'd make a wonderful mother
for my children," Chib says.

"The shock of Araby. Your Saturn has two moons,
mother and aunt. Chaperones! You say she'd make a good
mother! How good a wife! Is she intelligent?"

"She's as smart as Benedictine."

"A dumbshit then. You sure can pick them. How do
you know you're in love with her? You've been in love
with twenty women in the last six months."

"I love her. This is it."

"Until the next one. Can you really love anything but
your painting? Benedictine's going to have an abortion,
right?"

"Not if I can talk her out of it," Chib says. "To tell
the truth, I don't even like her any more. But she's carrying my child."

"Let me look at your pelvis. No, you're male. For a
moment, I wasn't sure, you're so crazy to have a baby."

"A baby is a miracle to stagger sextillions of infidels."

"It beats a mouse. But don't you know that Uncle Sam has been propagandizing his heart out to cut down on propagation? Where've you been all your life?"

"I got to go, Grandpa."

Chib kisses the old man and returns to his room to finish his latest painting. The door still refuses to recognize him, and he calls the gummint repair shop, only to be told that all technicians are at the Folk Festival. He leaves the house in a red rage. The bunting and balloons are waving and bobbing in the artificial wind, increased for this occasion, and an orchestra is playing by the lake.

Through the scope, Grandpa watches him walk away.

"Poor devil! I ache for his ache. He wants a baby, and he is ripped up inside because that poor devil Benedictine is aborting their child. Part of his agony, though he doesn't know it, is identification with the doomed infant. His own mother has had innumerable—well, quite a few—abortions. But for the grace of God, he would have been one of them, another nothingness. He wants this baby to have a chance, too. But there is nothing he can do about it, nothing.

"And there is another feeling, one which he shares with most of humankind. He knows he's screwed up his life, or something has twisted it. Every thinking man and woman knows this. Even the smug and dimwitted realize this unconsciously. But a baby, that beautiful being, that unsmirched blank tablet, unformed angel, represents a new hope. Perhaps it won't screw up. Perhaps it'll grow up to be a healthy confident reasonable good-humored unselfish loving man or woman. 'It won't be like me or my next-door neighbor,' the proud, but apprehensive, parent swears.

"Chib thinks this and swears that his baby will be different. But, like everybody else, he's fooling himself. A child has one father and mother, but it has trillions of aunts and uncles. Not only those that are its contemporaries; the dead, too. Even if Chib fled into the wilderness and raised the infant himself, he'd be giving it his own unconscious assumptions. The baby would grow up with beliefs and attitudes that the father was not even aware of. Moreover, being raised in isolation, the baby would be a very peculiar human being indeed.

"And if Chib raises the child in this society, it's inevitable that it will accept at least part of the attitudes of its playmates, teachers, and so on ad nauseam.

"So, forget about making a new Adam out of your wonderful potential-teeming child, Chib. If it grows up to become at least half-sane, it's because you gave it love and discipline and it was lucky in its social contacts and it was also blessed at birth with the right combination of genes. That is, your son or daughter is now both a fighter and a lover."

ONE MAN'S NIGHTMARE IS
ANOTHER MAN'S WET DREAM

Grandpa says.

"I was talking to Dante Alighieri just the other day, and he was telling me what an inferno of stupidity, cruelty, perversity, atheism, and outright peril the sixteenth century was. The nineteenth left him gibbering, hopelessly searching for adequate enough invectives.

"As for this age, it gave him such high-blood pressure, I had to slip him a tranquilizer and ship him out via time machine with an attendant nurse. She looked much like Beatrice and so should have been just the medicine he needed—maybe."

Grandpa chuckles, remembering that Chib, as a child, took him seriously, when he described his time-machine visitors, such notables as Nebuchadnezzar, King of the Grass-Eaters; Samson, Bronze Age Riddler and Scourge of the Philistines; Moses, who stole a god from his Kenite father-in-law and who fought against circumcision all his life; Buddha, the Original Beatnik; No-Moss Sisyphus, taking a vacation from his stone-rolling; Androcles and his buddy, the Cowardly Lion of Oz; Baron von Richthofen, the Red Knight of Germany; Beowulf; Al Capone; Hiawatha; Ivan the Terrible; and hundreds of others.

The time came when Grandpa became alarmed and decided that Chib was confusing fantasy with reality. He hated to tell the little boy that he had been making up all those wonderful stories, mostly to teach him history. It was like telling a kid there wasn't any Santa Claus.

And then, while he was reluctantly breaking the news to his grandson he became aware of Chib's barely suppressed grin and knew that it was his turn to have his leg pulled. Chib had never been fooled or else had caught on without any shock. So, both had a big laugh and Grandpa continued to tell of his visitors.

"There are no time machines," Grandpa says. "Like it or not, Miniver Cheevy, you have to live in this your time.

"The machines work in the utility-factory levels in a silence broken only by the chatter of a few mahouts. The great pipes at the bottom of the seas suck up water and bottom sludge. The stuff is automatically carried through pipes to the ten production levels of LA. There the inorganic chemicals are converted into energy and then into the matter of food, drink, medicines, and artifacts. There is very little agriculture or animal husbandry outside the city walls, but there is super-abundance for all. Artificial but exact duplication of organic stuff, so who knows the difference?

"There is no more starvation or want anywhere, except among the self-exiles wandering in the woods. And the food and goods are shipped to the pandoras and dispensed to the receivers of the purple wage. *The purple wage*. A Madison-Avenue euphemism with connotations of royalty and divine right. Earned by just being born.

"Other ages would regard ours as a delirium, yet ours has benefits others lacked. To combat transiency and rootlessness, the megalopolis is compartmented into small communities. A man can live all his life in one place without having to go elsewhere to get anything he needs. With this has come a provincialism, a small-town patriotism and hostility towards outsiders. Hence, the bloody juvenile gang-fights between towns. The intense and vicious gossip. The insistence on conformity to local mores.

"At the same time, the small-town citizen has fido, which enables him to see events anywhere in the world. Intermingled with the trash and the propaganda, which the government thinks is good for the people, is any amount of superb programs. A man may get the equivalent of a Ph.D. without stirring out of his house.

"Another Renaissance has come, a fruition of the arts comparable to that of Pericles' Athens and the city-states of Michelangelo's Italy or Shakespeare's England. Paradox. More illiterates than ever before in the world's history. But also more literates. Speakers of classical Latin outnumber those of Caesar's day. The world of aesthetics bears a fabulous fruit. And, of course, fruits.

"To dilute the provincialism and also to make international war even more unlikely, we have the world policy of *homogenization*. The voluntary exchange of a part of one nation's population with another's. Hostages to peace and brotherly love. Those citizens who can't get along on just the purple wage or who think they'll be happier elsewhere are inducted to emigrate with bribes.

"A Golden World in some respects; a nightmare in

others. So what's new with the world? It was always thus in every age. Ours has had to deal with overpopulation and automation. How else could the problem be solved? It's Buridan's ass (actually, the ass was a dog) all over again, as in every time. Buridan's ass, dying of hunger because it can't make up its mind which of two equal amounts of food to eat.

"History: *a pons asinorum* with men the asses on the bridge of time.

"No, those two comparisons are not fair or right. It's Hobson's horse, the only choice being the beast in the nearest stall. Zeitgeist rides tonight, and the devil take the hindmost!

"The mid-twentieth-century writers of the Triple Revolution document forecast accurately in some respects. But they de-emphasized what lack of work would do to Mr. Everyman. They believed that all men have equal potentialities in developing artistic tendencies, that all could busy themselves with arts, crafts, and hobbies or education for education's sake. They wouldn't face the 'undemocratic' reality that only about ten per cent of the population—if that—are inherently capable of producing anything worth while, or even mildly interesting, in the arts. Crafts, hobbies, and a lifelong academic education pale after a while, so back to the booze, fido, and adultery.

"Lacking self-respect, the fathers become free-floaters, nomads on the steppes of sex. Mother, with a capital M, becomes the dominant figure in the family. She may be playing around, too, but she's taking care of the kids; she's around most of the time. Thus, with father a lower-case figure, absent, weak, or indifferent, the children often become homosexual or ambisexual. The wonderland is also a fairyland.

"Some features of this time could have been predicted. Sexual permissiveness was one, although no one could have seen how far it would go. But then no one could have foreknown of the Panamorite sect, even if America has spawned lunatic-fringe cults as a frog spawns tadpoles. Yesterday's monomaniac is tomorrow's messiah, and so Sheltey and his disciples survived through years of persecution and today their precepts are embedded in our culture.''

Grandpa again fixes the cross-reticules of the scope on Chib.

''There he goes, my beautiful grandson, bearing gifts to the Greeks. So far, that Hercules has failed to clean up his psychic Augean stable. Yet, he may succeed, that stumblebum Apollo, that Edipus Wrecked. He's luckier than most of his contemporaries. He's had a permanent father, even if a secret one, a zany old man hiding from so-called justice. He has gotten love, discipline, and a superb education in this starred chamber. He's also fortunate in having a profession.

''But Mama spends far too much and also is addicted to gambling, a vice which deprives her of her full guaranteed income. I'm supposed to be dead, so I don't get the purple wage. Chib has to make up for all this by selling or trading his paintings. Luscus has helped him by publicizing him, but at any moment Luscus may turn against him. The money from the paintings is still not enough. After all, money is not the basis of our economy; it's a scarce auxiliary. Chib needs the grant but won't get it unless he lets Luscus make love to him.

''It's not that Chib rejects homosexual relations. Like most of his contemporaries, he's sexually ambivalent. I think that he and Omar Runic still blow each other occasionally. And why not? They love each other. But Chib rejects Luscus as a matter of principle. He won't be a whore to advance his career. Moreover, Chib makes a distinction which is deeply embedded in this society. He thinks that uncompulsive homosexuality is natural (whatever that means?) but that compulsive homosexuality is, to use an old term, queer. Valid or not, the distinction is made.

"So, Chib may go to Egypt. But what happens to me then?

"Never mind me or your mother, Chib. No matter what. Don't give in to Luscus. Remember the dying words of Singleton, Bureau of Relocation and Rehabilitation Director, who shot himself because he couldn't adjust to the new times.

" 'What if a man gain the world and lose his ass?' "

At this moment, Grandpa sees his grandson, who has been walking along with somewhat drooping shoulders, suddenly straighten them. And he sees Chib break into a dance, a little improvised shuffle followed by a series of whirls. It is evident that Chib is whooping. The pedestrians around him are grinning.

Grandpa groans and then laughs. "Oh, God, the goatish energy of youth, the unpredictable shift of spectrum from black sorrow to bright orange joy! Dance, Chib, dance your crazy head off! Be happy, if only for a moment! You're young yet, you've got the bubbling of unconquerable hope deep in your springs! Dance, Chib, dance!"

He laughs and wipes a tear away.

SEXUAL IMPLICATIONS OF THE CHARGE OF THE LIGHT BRIGADE

is so fascinating a book that Doctor Jespersen Joyce Bathymens, psycholinguist for the federal Bureau of Group Reconfiguration and Intercommunicability, hates to stop reading. But duty beckons.

"A radish is not necessarily reddish," he says into the recorder. "The Young Radishes so named their group because a radish is a radicle, hence, radical. Also, there's a play on roots and on red-ass, a slang term for anger, and possibly on ruttish and rattish. And undoubtedly on rude-ickle, Beverly Hills dialectical term for a repulsive, unruly, and socially ungraceful person.

"Yet the Young Radishes are not what I would call Left Wing; they represent the current resentment against Life-In-General and advocate no radical policy of reconstruction. They howl against Things As They Are, like monkeys in a tree, but never give constructive criticism. They want to destroy without any thought of what to do after the destruction.

"In short, they represent the average citizen's grousing and bitching, being different in that they are more articulate. There are thousands of groups like them in LA and possibly millions all over the world. They had a normal life as children. In fact, they were born and raised in the same clutch, which is one reason why they were chosen for this study. What phenomenon produced ten such creative persons, all mothered in the seven houses of Area 69-14, all about the same time, all practically raised together, since they were put together in the playpen on top of the pedestal while one mother took her turn baby-sitting and the others did whatever they had to do, which . . . where was I?

"Oh, yes, they had a normal life, went to the same school, palled around, enjoyed the usual sexual play among themselves, joined the juvenile gangs and engaged in some rather bloody warfare with the Westwood and other gangs. All were distinguished, however, by an intense intellectual curiosity and all became active in the creative arts.

"It has been suggested—and might be true—that the mysterious stranger, Raleigh Renaissance, was the father of all ten. This is possible but can't be proved. Raleigh Renaissance was living in the house of Mrs. Winnegan at the time, but he seems to have been unusually active in the clutch, and, indeed, all over Beverly Hills. Where this man came from, who he was, and where he went are still unknown despite intensive search by various agencies. He had no ID or other cards of any kind yet he went unchallenged for a long time. He seems to have had something on the Chief of Police of Beverly Hills and possibly on some of the federal agents stationed in Beverly Hills.

"He lived for two years with Mrs. Winnegan, then dropped out of sight. It is rumored that he left LA to join a tribe of white neo-Amerinds, sometimes called the Seminal Indians.

"Anyway, back to the Young (pun on Jung?) Radishes. They are revolting against the Father Image of Uncle Sam, whom they both love and hate. Uncle is, of course, linked by their subconsciouses with *unco*, a Scottish word meaning strange, uncanny, weird, this indicating that their own fathers were strangers to them. All come from homes where the father was missing or weak, a phenomenon regrettably common in our culture.

"I never knew my own father . . . Tooney, wipe that out as irrelevant. *Unco* also means news or tidings, indicating that the unfortunate young men are eagerly awaiting news of the return of their fathers and perhaps secretly hoping for reconciliation with Uncle Sam, that is, their fathers.

"Uncle Sam. Sam is short for Samuel, from the Hebrew *Shemu'el*, meaning Name of God. All the Radishes are atheists, although some, notably Omar Runic and Chibiabos Winnegan, were given religious instruction as children (Panamorite and Roman Catholic, respectively).

"Young Winnegan's revolt against God, and against the Catholic Church, was undoubtedly reinforced by the fact that his mother forced strong *cath*artics upon him when he had a chronic constipation. He probably also resented having to learn his *cate*chism when he preferred to play. And there is the deeply significant and traumatic incident in which a *cath*eter was used on him. (This refusal to excrete when young will be analyzed in a later report.)

"Uncle Sam, the Father Figure. *Figure* is so obvious a play that I won't bother to point it out. Also perhaps on *figger*, in the sense of 'a fig on thee!'—look this up in Dante's *Inferno*, some Italian or other in Hell said, 'A fig on thee, God!' biting his thumb in the ancient gesture of defiance and disrespect. Hmm? Biting the thumb—an infantile characteristic?

"Sam is also a multileveled pun on phonetically, orthographically, and semisemantically linked words. It is significant that young Winnegan can't stand to be called *dear*; he claims that his mother called him that so many times it nauseates him. Yet the word has a deeper meaning to him. For instance, *sambar* is an Asiatic *deer* with *three*-pointed antlers. (Note the *sam*, also.) Obviously, the three points symbolize, to him, the Triple Revolution document, the historic dating point of the beginning of our era, which Chib claims to hate so. The three points are also archetypes of the Holy Trinity, which the Young Radishes frequently blaspheme against.

"I might point out that in this the group differs from others I've studied. The others expressed an infrequent and mild blasphemy in keeping with the mild, indeed pale, religious spirit prevalent nowadays. Strong blasphemers thrive only when strong believers thrive.

"Sam also stands for *same*, indicating the Radishes' subconscious desire to conform.

"Possibly, although this particular analysis may be invalid, Sam corresponds to Samekh, the fifteenth letter of the Hebrew alphabet. (Sam! Ech!?) In the old style of

English spelling, which the Radishes learned in their childhood, the fifteenth letter of the Roman alphabet is O. In the Alphabet Table of my dictionary, Webster's 128th New Collegiate, the Roman O is in the same horizontal column as the Arabic Dad. Also with the Hebrew Mem. So we get a double connection with the missing and longed for Father (or Dad) and with the overdominating Mother (or Mem).

"I can make nothing out of the Greek Omicron, also in the same horizontal column. But give me time; this takes study.

"Omicron. The little O! The lower-case omicron has an egg shape. The little egg is their father's sperm fertilized? The womb? The basic shape of modern architecture?

"Sam Hill, an archaic euphemism for Hell. Uncle Sam is a Sam Hill of a father? Better strike that out, Tooney. It's possible that these highly educated youths have read about this obsolete phrase, but it's not confirmable. I don't want to suggest any connections that might make me look ridiculous.

"Let's see. Samisen. A Japanese musical instrument with *three* strings. The Triple Revolution document and the Trinity again. Trinity? Father, Son, and Holy Ghost. Mother the thoroughly despised figure, hence, the Wholly Goose? Well, maybe not. Wipe that out, Tooney.

"Samisen. Son of Sam? Which leads naturally to Samson, who pulled down the temple of the Philistines on them and on himself. These boys talk of doing the same thing. Chuckle. Reminds me of myself when I was their age, before I matured. Strike out that last remark, Tooney.

"Samovar. The Russian word means, literally, self-boiler. There's no doubt the Radishes are boiling with revolutionary fervor. Yet their disturbed psyches know, deep down, that Uncle Sam is their everloving Father-

Mother, that he has only their best interests at heart. But they force themselves to hate him, hence, they self-boil.

"A samlet is a young salmon. Cooked salmon is a yellowish pink or pale red, near to a radish in color, in their unconsciouses, anyway. Samlet equals Young Radish; they feel they're being cooked in the great pressure cooker of modern society.

"How's that for a trinely furned phase—I mean, finely turned phrase, Tooney? Run this off, edit as indicated, smooth it out, you know how, and send it off to the boss. I got to go. I'm late for lunch with Mother; she gets very upset if I'm not there on the dot.

"Oh, postscript! I recommend that the agents watch Winnegan more closely. His friends are blowing off psychic steam through talk and drink, but he has suddenly altered his behavior pattern. He has long periods of silence, he's given up smoking, drinking, and sex."

A PROFIT IS NOT WITHOUT HONOR

even in this day. The gummint has no overt objection to privately owned taverns, run by citizens who have paid all license fees, passed all examinations, posted all bonds, and bribed the local politicians and police chief. Since there is no provision made for them, no large buildings available for rent, the taverns are in the homes of the owners themselves.

The Private Universe is Chib's favorite, partly because the proprietor is operating illegally. Dionysus Gobrinus, unable to hew his way through the roadblocks, prise-de-chevaux, barbed wire, and booby-traps of official procedure, has quit his efforts to get a license.

Openly, he paints the name of his establishment over the mathematical equations that once distinguished the exterior of the house. (Math prof at Beverly Hills U. 14, named Al-Khwarizmi Descartes Lobachevsky, he has resigned and changed his name again.) The atrium and several bedrooms have been converted for drinking and carousing. There are no Egyptian customers, probably because of their supersensitivity about the flowery sentiments painted by patrons on the inside walls.

A BAS, ABU

MOHAMMED WAS THE SON OF A VIRGIN DOG

THE SPHINX STINKS

REMEMBER THE RED SEA!

THE PROPHET HAS A CAMEL FETISH

Some of those who wrote the taunts have fathers, grandfathers, and great-grandfathers who were themselves the objects of similar insults. But their descendants are thoroughly assimilated, Beverly Hillsians to the core. Of such is the kingdom of men.

Gobrinus, a squat cube of a man, stands behind the bar, which is square as a protest against the ovoid. Above him is a big sign:

ONE MAN'S MEAD IS
ANOTHER MAN'S POISSON

Gobrinus has explained this pun many times, not always to his listener's satisfaction. Suffice it that Poisson was a mathematician and that Poisson's frequency distribution is a good approximation to the binomial distribution as the number of trials increases and probability of success in a single trial is small.

When a customer gets too drunk to be permitted one more drink, he is hurled headlong from the tavern with furious combustion and utter ruin by Gobrinus, who cries, "Poisson! Poisson!"

Chib's friends, the Young Radishes, sitting at a hexagonal table, greet him, and their words unconsciously echo those of the federal psycholinguist's estimate of his recent behavior.

"Chib, monk! Chibber as ever! Looking for a chibbie, no doubt! Take your pick!"

Madame Trismegista, sitting at a little table with a Seal-of-Solomon-shape top, greets him. She has been Gobrinus' wife for two years, a record, because she will knife him if he leaves her. Also, he believes that she can somehow juggle his destiny with the cards she deals. In this age of enlightenment, the soothsayer and astrologer flourish. As science pushes forward, ignorance and superstition gallop around the flanks and bite science in the rear with big dark teeth.

Gobrinus himself, a Ph.D., holder of the torch of knowledge (until lately, anyway), does not believe in God. But he is sure the stars are marching towards a baleful conjunction for him. With a strange logic, he thinks that his wife's cards control the stars; he is unaware that card-divination and astrology are entirely separate fields.

What can you expect of a man who claims that the universe is asymmetric?

Chib waves his hand at Madame Trismegista and walks to another table. Here sits

A TYPICAL TEEMAGER

Benedictine Serinus Melba. She is tall and slim and has narrow lemurlike hips and slender legs but big breasts. Her hair, black as the pupils of her eyes, is parted in the middle, plastered with perfumed spray to the skull, and braided into two long pigtails. These are brought over her bare shoulders and held together with a golden brooch just below her throat. From the brooch, which is in the form of a musical note, the braids part again, one looping under each breast. Another brooch secures them, and they separate to circle behind her back, are brooched again, and come back to meet on her belly. Another brooch holds them, and the twin waterfalls flow blackly over the front of her bell-shaped skirt.

Her face is thickly farded with green, aquamarine, a shamrock beauty mark, and topaz. She wears a yellow bra with artificial pink nipples; frilly lace ribbons hang from the bra. A demicorselet of bright green with black rosettes circles her waist. Over the corselet, half-concealing it, is a wire structure covered with a shimmering pink quilty material. It extends out in back to form a semifuselage or a bird's long tail, to which are attached long yellow and crimson artificial feathers.

An ankle-length diaphanous skirt billows out. It does not hide the yellow and dark-green striped lace-fringed garter-panties, white thighs, and black net stockings with green clocks in the shape of musical notes. Her shoes are bright blue with topaz high heels.

Benedictine is costumed to sing at the Folk Festival; the only thing missing is her singer's hat. Yet, she came to complain, among other things, that Chib has forced her to cancel her appearance and so lose her chance at a great career.

She is with five girls, all between sixteen and twenty-one, all drinking P (for popskull).

"Can't we talk in private, Benny?" Chib says.

"What for?" Her voice is a lovely contralto ugly with inflection.

"You got me down here to make a public scene," Chib says.

"For God's sake, what other kind of scene is there?" she shrills. "Look at him! He wants to talk to me alone!"

It is then that he realizes she is afraid to be alone with him. More than that, she is incapable of being alone. Now he knows why she insisted on leaving the bedroom door open with her girl-friend, Bela, within calling distance. And listening distance.

"You said you was just going to use your finger!" she shouts. She points at the slightly rounded belly. "I'm going to have a baby! You rotten smooth-talking sick bastard!"

"That isn't true at all," Chib says. "You told me it was all right, you loved me."

" 'Love! Love!' he says! What the hell do I know what I said, you got me so excited! Anyway, I didn't say you could stick it in! I'd never say that, never! And then what you *did*! *What* you did! My God, I could hardly walk for a week, you bastard, you!"

Chib sweats. Except for Beethoven's Pastoral welling from the fido, the room is silent. His friends grin. Gobrinus, his back turned, is drinking scotch. Madame Trismegista shuffles her cards, and she farts with a fiery conjunction of beer and onions. Benedictine's friends look at their Mandarin-long fluorescent fingernails or glare at him. Her hurt and indignity is theirs and vice versa.

"I can't take those pills. They make me break out and

give me eye trouble and screw up my monthlies! You know that! And I can't stand those mechanical uteruses! And you lied to me anyway! You said you took a pill!''

Chib realizes she's contradicting herself, but there's no use trying to be logical. She's furious because she's pregnant; she doesn't want to be inconvenienced with an abortion at this time, and she's out for revenge.

Now how, Chib wonders, how could she get pregnant *that* night? No woman, no matter how fertile, could have managed that. She must have been knocked up before or after. Yet she swears that it was that night, the night he was

THE KNIGHT OF THE BURNING PESTLE
OR
FOAM, FOAM ON THE RANGE

''No, no!'' Benedictine cries.

''Why not? I love you,'' Chib says. ''I want to marry you.''

Benedictine screams, and her friend Bela, out in the hall, yells, ''What's the matter? What happened?''

Benedictine does not reply. Raging, shaking as if in the grip of a fever, she scrambles out of bed, pushing Chib to one side. She runs to the small egg of the bathroom in the corner, and he follows her.

''I hope you're not going to do what I think . . . ?'' he says.

Benedictine moans, ''You sneaky no-good son of a bitch!''

In the bathroom, she pulls down a section of wall, which becomes a shelf. On its top, attached by magnetic bottoms to the shelf, are many containers. She seizes a long thin can of spermatocide, squats, and inserts it. She presses the button on its bottom, and it foams with a hissing sound even its cover of flesh cannot silence.

Chib is paralyzed for a moment. Then he roars.

Benedictine shouts, "Stay away from me, you rude-ickle!"

From the door to the bedroom comes Bela's timid, "Are you all right, Benny?"

"I'll all-right her!" Chib bellows.

He jumps forward and takes a can of tempoxy glue from the shelf. The glue is used by Benedictine to attach her wigs to her head and will hold anything forever unless softened by a specific defixative.

Benedictine and Bela both cry out as Chib lifts Benedictine up and then lowers her to the floor. She fights, but he manages to spray the glue over the can and the skin and hairs around it.

"What're you doing?" she screams.

He pushes the button on the can to full-on position and then sprays the bottom with glue. While she struggles, he holds her arms tight against her body and keeps her from rolling over and so moving the can in or out. Silently, Chib counts to thirty, then to thirty more to make sure the glue is thoroughly dried. He releases her.

The foam is billowing out around her groin and down her legs and spreading out across the floor. The fluid in the can is under enormous pressure in the indestructible unpunchable can, and the foam expands vastly if exposed to open air.

Chib takes the can of defixative from the shelf and clutches it in his hand, determined that she will not have it. Benedictine jumps up and swings at him. Laughing like a hyena in a tentful of nitrous oxide, Chib blocks her fist and shoves her away. Slipping on the foam, which is ankle-deep by now, Benedictine falls and then slides backward out of the bedroom on her buttocks, the can clunking.

She gets to her feet and only then realizes fully what Chib has done. Her scream goes up, and she follows it. She dances around, yanking at the can, her screams intensifying with every tug and resultant pain. Then she turns and runs out of the room or tries to. She skids; Bela is in her way; they cling together and both ski out of the room, doing a half-turn while going through the door. The foam swirls out so that the two look like Venus and friend rising from the bubble-capped waves of the Cyprian Sea.

Benedictine shoves Bela away but not without losing some flesh to Bela's long sharp fingernails. Bela shoots backwards through the door toward Chib. She is like a novice ice skater trying to maintain her balance. She does not succeed and shoots by Chib, wailing, on her back, her feet up in the air.

Chib slides his bare feet across the floor gingerly, stops at the bed to pick up his clothes, but decides he'd be wiser to wait until he's outside before he puts them on. He gets to the circular hall just in time to see Benedictine crawling past one of the columns that divides the corridor from the atrium. Her parents, two middle-aged behemoths, are still sitting on a flato, beer cans in hand, eyes wide, mouths open, quivering.

Chib does not even say goodnight to them as he passes along the hall. But then he sees the fido and realizes that her parents had switched it from EXT. to INT. and then to Benedictine's room. Father and mother have been watching Chib and daughter and it is evident from father's not-quite dwindled condition that father was very excited by this show, superior to anything seen on exterior fido.

"You peeping bastards!" Chib roars.

Benedictine has gotten to them and on her feet and she

is stammering, weeping, indicating the can and then stabbing her finger at Chib. At Chib's roar, the parents heave up from the flato as two leviathans from the deep. Benedictine turns and starts to run towards him, her arms outstretched, her long-nailed fingers curved, her face a medusa's. Behind her streams the wake of the livid witch and father and mother on the foam.

Chib shoves up against a pillar and rebounds and skitters off, helpless to keep himself from turning sidewise during the maneuver. But he keeps his balance. Mama and Papa have gone down together with a crash that shakes even the solid house. They are up, eyes rolling and bellowing like hippos surfacing. They charge him but separate, Mama shrieking now, her face, despite the fat, Benedictine's. Papa goes around one side of the pillar; Mama, the other. Benedictine has rounded another pillar, holding to it with one hand to keep her from slipping. She is between Chib and the door to the outside.

Chib slams against the wall of the corridor, in an area free of foam. Benedictine runs towards him. He dives across the floor, hits it, and rolls between two pillars and out into the atrium.

Mama and Papa converge in a collision course. The Titanic meets the iceberg, and both plunge swiftly. They skid on their faces and bellies towards Benedictine. She leaps into the air, trailing foam on them as they pass beneath her.

By now it is evident that the government's claim that the can is good for 40,000 shots of death-to-sperm, or for 40,000 copulations, is justified. Foam is all over the place ankle-deep—knee-high in some places—and still pouring out.

Bela is on her back now and on the atrium floor, her head driven into the soft folds of the flato.

Chib gets up slowly and stands for a moment, glaring around him, his knees bent, ready to jump from danger but hoping he won't have to since his feet will undoubtedly fly away from under him.

"Hold it, you rotten son of a bitch!" Papa roars. "I'm going to kill you! You can't do this to my daughter!"

Chib watches him turn over like a whale in a heavy sea and try to get to his feet. Down he goes again, grunting as if hit by a harpoon. Mama is no more successful than he.

Seeing that his way is unbarred—Benedictine having disappeared somewhere—Chib skis across the atrium until he reaches an unfoamed area near the exit. Clothes over his arm, still holding the defixative, he struts towards the door.

At this moment Benedictine calls his name. He turns to see her sliding from the kitchen at him. In her hand is a tall glass. He wonders what she intends to do with it. Certainly, she is not offering him the hospitality of a drink.

Then she scoots into the dry region of the floor and topples forward with a scream. Nevertheless, she throws the contents of the glass accurately.

Chib screams when he feels the boiling hot water, painful as if he had been circumcised unanesthetized.

Benedictine, on the floor, laughs. Chib, after jumping around and shrieking, the can and clothes dropped, his hands holding the scalded parts, manages to control himself. He stops his antics, seizes Benedictine's right hand, and drags her out into the streets of Beverly Hills. There are quite a few people out this night, and they follow the two. Not until Chib reaches the lake does he stop and there he goes into the water to cool off the burn, Benedictine with him.

The crowd has much to talk about later, after Benedictine and Chib have crawled out of the lake and then run home. The crowd talks and laughs quite a while as they watch the sanitation department people clean the foam off the lake surface and the streets.

"I was so sore I couldn't walk for a month!" Benedictine screams.

"You had it coming," Chib says. "You've got no complaints. You said you wanted my baby, and you talked as if you meant it."

"I must've been out of my mind!" Benedictine says. "No, I wasn't! I never said no such thing! You lied to me! You forced me!"

"I would never force anybody," Chib said. "You know that. Quit your bitching. You're a free agent, and you consented freely. You have free will."

Omar Runic, the poet, stands up from his chair. He is a tall thin red-bronze youth with an aquiline nose and very thick red lips. His kinky hair grows long and is cut into the shape of the *Pequod*, that fabled vessel which bore mad Captain Ahab and his mad crew and the sole survivor Ishmael after the white whale. The coiffure is formed with a bowsprit and hull and three masts and yardarms and even a boat hanging on davits.

Omar Runic claps his hands and shouts, "Bravo! A philosopher! Free will it is; free will to seek the Eternal Verities—if any—or Death and Damnation! I'll drink to free will! A toast, gentlemen! Stand up, Young Radishes, a toast to our leader!"

And so begins

THE MAD P PARTY

Madame Trismegista calls, "Tell your fortune, Chib! See what the stars tell through the cards!"

He sits down at her table while his friends crowd around.

"O.K., Madame. How do I get out of this mess?"

She shuffles and turns over the top card.

"Jesus! The ace of spades!"

"You're going on a long journey!"

"Egypt!" Rousseau Red Hawk cries. "Oh, no, you don't want to go there, Chib! Come with me to where the buffalo roam and . . ."

Up comes another card.

"You will soon meet a beautiful dark lady."

"A goddam Arab! Oh, no, Chib, tell me it's not true!"

"You will win great honors soon."

"Chib's going to get the grant!"

"If I get the grant, I don't have to go to Egypt," Chib says. "Madame Trismegista, with all due respect, you're full of crap."

"Don't mock, young man. I'm not a computer. I'm tuned to the spectrum of psychic vibrations."

Flip. "You will be in great danger, physically and morally."

Chib says, "That happens at least once a day."

Flip. "A man very close to you will die twice."

Chib pales, rallies, and says, "A coward dies a thousand deaths."

"You will travel in time, return to the past."

"Zow!" Red Hawk says. "You're outdoing yourself,

Madame. Careful! You'll get a psychic hernia, have to wear an ectoplasmic truss!''

"Scoff if you want to, you dumbshits," Madame says. "There are more worlds than one. The cards don't lie, not when I deal them."

"Gobrinus!" Chib calls. "Another pitcher of beer for the Madame."

The Young Radishes return to their table, a legless disc held up in the air by a graviton field. Benedictine glares at them and goes into a huddle with the other teemagers. At a table nearby sits Pinkerton Legrand, a gummint agent, facing them so that the fido under his one-way window of a jacket beams in on them. They know he's doing this. He knows they know and has reported so to his superior. He frowns when he sees Falco Accipiter enter. Legrand does not like an agent from another department messing around on his case. Accipiter does not even look at Legrand. He orders a pot of tea and then pretends to drop into the teapot a pill that combines with tannic acid to become P.

Rousseau Red Hawk winks at Chib and says, "Do you really think it's possible to paralyze all of LA with a single bomb?"

"Three bombs!" Chib says loudly so that Legrand's fido will pick up the words. "One for the control console of the desalinization plant, a second for the backup console, the third for the nexus of the big pipe that carries the water to the reservoir on the 20th level."

Pinkerton Legrand turns pale. He downs all the whiskey in his glass and orders another, although he has already had too many. He presses the plate on his fido to transmit a triple top-priority. Lights blink redly in HQ; a gong clangs repeatedly; the chief wakes up so suddenly he falls off his chair.

Accipiter also hears, but he sits stiff, dark, and brooding as the diorite image of a Pharaoh's falcon. Monomaniac, he is not to be diverted by talk of inundating all LA, even if it will lead to action. On Grandpa's trail, he is now here because he hopes to use Chib as the key to the house. One ''mouse''—as he thinks of his criminals—one ''mouse'' will run to the hole of another.

''When do you think we can go into action?'' Huga Wells-Erb Heinsturbury, the science-fiction authoress, says.

''In about three weeks,'' Chib says.

At HQ, the chief curses Legrand for disturbing him. There are thousands of young men and women blowing off steam with these plots of destruction, assassination, and revolt. He does not understand why the young punks talk like this, since they have everything handed them free. If he had his way, he'd throw them into jail and kick them around a little or more than.

''After we do it, we'll have to take off for the big outdoors,'' Red Hawk says. His eyes glisten. ''I'm telling you, boys, being a free man in the forest is the greatest. You're a genuine individual, not just one of the faceless breed.''

Red Hawk believes in this plot to destroy LA. He is happy because, though he hasn't said so, he has grieved while in Mother Nature's lap for intellectual companionship. The other savages can hear a deer at a hundred yards, detect a rattlesnake in the bushes, but they're deaf to the footfalls of philosophy, the neigh of Nietzsche, the rattle of Russell, the honkings of Hegel.

''The illiterate swine!'' he says aloud. The others say, ''What?''

''Nothing. Listen, you guys must know how wonderful it is. You were in the WNRCC.''

''I was 4-F,'' Omar Runic says. ''I got hay fever.''

''I was working on my second M.A.,'' Gibbon Tacitus says.

"I was in the WNRCC band," Sibelius Amadeus Yehudi says. "We only got outside when we played the camps, and that wasn't often."

"Chib, you were in the Corps. You loved it, didn't you?"

Chib nods but says, "Being a neo-Amerind takes all your time just to survive. When could I paint? And who would see the paintings if I did get time? Anyway, that's no life for a woman or a baby."

Red Hawk looks hurt and orders a whiskey mixed with P.

Pinkerton Legrand doesn't want to interrupt his monitoring, yet he can't stand the pressure in his bladder. He walks towards the room used as the customers' catch-all. Red Hawk, in a nasty mood caused by rejection, sticks his leg out. Legrand trips, catches himself, and stumbles forward. Benedictine puts out her leg. Legrand falls on his face. He no longer has any reason to go to the urinal except to wash himself off.

Everybody except Legrand and Accipiter laugh. Legrand jumps up, his fists doubled. Benedictine ignores him and walks over to Chib, her friends following. Chib stiffens. She says, "You perverted bastard! You told me you were just going to use your finger!"

"You're repeating yourself," Chib says. "The important thing is, what's going to happen to the baby?"

"What do you care?" Benedictine says. "For all you know, it might not even be yours!"

"That'd be a relief," Chib says, "if it weren't. Even so, the baby should have a say in this. He might want to live—even with you as his mother."

"In this miserable life!" she cries. "I'm going to do it a favor. I'm going to the hospital and get rid of it. Because of you, I have to miss out on my big chance at the Folk Festival! There'll be agents from all over there, and I won't get a chance to sing for them!''

''You're a liar,'' Chib says. ''You're all dressed up to sing.''

Benedictine's face is red; her eyes, wide; her nostrils, flaring.

''You spoiled my fun!''

She shouts, ''Hey, everybody, want to hear a howler! This great artist, this big hunk of manhood, Chib the divine, he can't get a hard-on unless he's gone down on!''

Chib's friends look at each other. What's the bitch screaming about? So what's new?

From Grandpa's *Private Ejaculations*:

Some of the features of the Panamorite religion, so reviled and loathed in the 21st century, have become everyday facts in modern times. Love, love, love, physical and spiritual! It's not enough to just kiss your children and hug them. But oral stimulation of the genitals of infants by the parents and relatives has resulted in some curious conditioned reflexes. I could write a book about this aspect of mid-22nd century life and probably will.

Legrand comes out of the washroom. Benedictine slaps Chib's face. Chib slaps her back. Gobrinus lifts up a section of the bar and hurtles through the opening, crying, ''Poisson! Poisson!''

He collides with Legrand, who lurches into Bela, who screams, whirls, and slaps Legrand, who slaps back. Benedictine empties a glass of P in Chib's face. Howling, he jumps up and swings his fist. Benedictine ducks, and the fist goes over her shoulder into a girl-friend's chest.

Red Hawk leaps up on the table and shouts, "I'm a regular bearcat, half-alligator and half . . ."

The table, held up in a graviton field, can't bear much weight. It tilts and catapults him into the girls, and all go down. They bite and scratch Red Hawk, and Benedictine squeezes his testicles. He screams, writhes, and hurls Benedictine with his feet onto the top of the table. It has regained its normal height and altitude, but now it flips over again, tossing her to the other side. Legrand, tippytoeing through the crowd on his way to the exit, is knocked down. He loses some front teeth against somebody's knee cap. Spitting blood and teeth, he jumps up and slugs a bystander.

Gobrinus fires off a gun that shoots a tiny Very light. It's supposed to blind the brawlers and so bring them to their senses while they're regaining their sight. It hangs in the air and shines like

A STAR OVER BEDLAM

The Police Chief is talking via fido to a man in a public booth. The man has turned off the video and is disguising his voice.

"They're beating the shit out of each other in The Private Universe."

The Chief groans. The Festival has just begun, and They are at it already.

"Thanks. The boys'll be on the way. What's your name? I'd like to recommend you for a Citizen's Medal."

"What! And get the shit knocked out of me, too! I ain't no stoolie; just doing my duty. Besides, I don't like Gobrinus or his customers. They're a bunch of snobs."

The Chief issues orders to the riot squad, leans back,

and drinks a beer while he watches the operation on fido. What's the matter with these people, anyway? They're always mad about something.

The sirens scream. Although the bolgani ride electrically driven noiseless tricycles, they're still clinging to the centuries-old tradition of warning the criminals that they're coming. Five trikes pull up before the open door of The Private Universe. The police dismount and confer. Their two-storied cylindrical helmets are black and have scarlet roaches. They wear goggles for some reason although their vehicles can't go over 15 m.p.h. Their jackets are black and fuzzy, like a teddy bear's fur, and huge golden epaulets decorate their shoulders. The shorts are electric-blue and fuzzy; the jackboots, glossy black. They carry electric shock sticks and guns that fire chokegas pellets.

Gobrinus blocks the entrance. Sergeant O'Hara says, "Come on, let us in. No, I don't have a warrant of entry. But I'll get one."

"If you do, I'll sue," Gobrinus says. He smiles. While it is true that government red tape was so tangled he quit trying to acquire a tavern legally, it is also true that the government will protect him in this issue. Invasion of privacy is a tough rap for the police to break.

O'Hara looks inside the doorway at the two bodies on the floor, at those holding their heads and sides and wiping off blood, and at Accipiter, sitting like a vulture dreaming of carrion. One of the bodies gets up on all fours and crawls through between Gobrinus' legs out into the street.

"Sergeant, arrest that man!" Gobrinus says. "He's wearing an illegal fido. I accuse him of invasion of privacy."

O'Hara's face lights up. At least he'll get one arrest to his credit. Legrand is placed in the paddywagon, which arrives just after the ambulance. Red Hawk is carried out as far as the doorway by his friends. He opens his eyes just as he's being carried on a stretcher to the ambulance and he mutters.

O'Hara leans over him. "What?"

"I fought a bear once with only my knife, and I came out better than with those cunts. I charge them with assault and battery, murder and mayhem."

O'Hara's attempt to get Red Hawk to sign a warrant fails because Red Hawk is now unconscious. He curses. By the time Red Hawk begins feeling better, he'll refuse to sign the warrant. He won't want the girls and their boy-friends laying for him, not if he has any sense at all.

Through the barred window of the paddywagon, Legrand screams, "I'm a gummint agent! You can't arrest me!"

The police get a hurry-up call to go to the front of the Folk Center, where a fight between local youths and Westwood invaders is threatening to become a riot. Benedictine leaves the tavern. Despite several blows in the shoulders and stomach, a kick in the buttocks, and a bang on the head, she shows no sign of losing the fetus.

Chib, half-sad, half-glad, watches her go. He feels a dull grief that the baby is to be denied life. By now he realizes that part of his objection to the abortion is identification with the fetus; he knows what Grandpa thinks he does not know. He realizes that his birth was an accident—lucky or unlucky. If things had gone otherwise, he would not have been born. The thought of his non-existence—no painting, no friends, no laughter, no hope, no love—horrifies him. His mother, drunkenly negligent about contraception, has had any number of abortions, and he could have been one of them.

Watching Benedictine swagger away (despite her torn clothes), he wonders what he could ever have seen in her. Life with her, even with a child, would have been gritty.

In the hope-lined nest of the mouth
Love flies once more, nestles down,
Coos, flashes feathered glory, dazzles,
And then flies away, crapping,
As is the wont of birds,
To jet-assist the take off.

—Omar Runic

Chib returns to his home, but he still can't get back into his room. He goes to the storeroom. The painting is seven-eighths finished but was not completed because he was dissatisfied with it. Now he takes it from the house and carries it to Runic's house, which is in the same clutch as his. Runic is at the Center, but he always leaves his doors open when he's gone. He has equipment which Chib uses to finish the painting, working with a sureness and intensity he lacked the first time he was creating it. He then leaves Runic's house with the huge oval canvas held above his head.

He strides past the pedestals and under their curving branches with the ovoids at their ends. He skirts several small grassy parks with trees, walks beneath more houses, and in ten minutes is nearing the heart of Beverly Hills. Here mercurial Chib sees

ALL IN THE GOLDEN AFTERNOON, THREE LEADEN LADIES

drifting in a canoe on Lake Issus. Maryam bint Yusuf, her mother, and aunt listlessly hold fishing poles and look towards the gay colors, music, and the chattering crowd before the Folk Center. By now the police have broken up the juvenile fight and are standing around to make sure nobody else makes trouble.

The three women are dressed in the somber clothes, completely body-concealing, of the Mohammedan Wahhabi fundamentalist sect. They do not wear veils; not even the Wahhabi now insist on this. Their Egyptian brethren ashore are clad in modern garments, shameful and sinful. Despite which, the ladies stare at them.

Their menfolk are at the edge of the crowd. Bearded and costumed like sheiks in a Foreign Legion fido show, they mutter gargling oaths and hiss at the iniquitous display of female flesh. But they stare.

This small group has come from the zoological preserves of Abyssinia, where they were caught poaching. Their gummint gave them three choices. Imprisonment in a rehabilitation center, where they would be treated until they became good citizens if it took the rest of their lives. Emigration to the megalopolis of Haifa, Israel. Or emigration to Beverly Hills, LA.

What, dwell among the accursed Jews of Israel? They spat and chose Beverly Hills. Alas, Allah had mocked them! They were now surrounded by Finkelsteins, Applebaums, Siegels, Weintraubs, and others of the infidel tribes of Isaac. Even worse, Beverly Hills had no mosque. They either traveled forty kilometers every day to the 16th level, where a mosque was available, or used a private home.

Chib hastens to the edge of the plastic-edged lake and puts down his painting and bows low, whipping off his somewhat battered hat. Maryam smiles at him but loses the smile when the two chaperones reprimand her.

"Ya kelb! Ya ibn kelb!" the two shout at him.

Chib grins at them, waves his hat, and says, "Charmed, I'm sure, mesdames! Oh, you lovely ladies remind me of the Three Graces."

He then cries out, "I love you, Maryam! I love you!

Thou art like the Rose of Sharon to me! Beautiful, doe-eyed, virginal! A fortress of innocence and strength, filled with a fierce motherhood and utter faithfulness to the one true love! I love thee, thou art the only light in a black sky of dead stars! I cry to you across the void!''

Maryam understands World English, but the wind carries his words away from her. She simpers, and Chib cannot help feeling a momentary repulsion, a flash of anger as if she has somehow betrayed him. Nevertheless, he rallies and shouts, ''I invite you to come with me to the showing! You and your mother and aunt will be my guests. You can see my paintings, my soul, and know what kind of man is going to carry you off on his Pegasus, my dove!''

There is nothing as ridiculous as the verbal out-pourings of a young poet in love. Outrageously exaggerated. I laugh. But I am also touched. Old as I am, I remember my first loves, the fires, the torrents of words, lightning-sheathed, ache-winged. Dear lasses, most of you are dead; the rest, withered. I blow you a kiss.

—Grandpa

Maryam's mother stands up in the canoe. For a second, her profile is to Chib, and he sees intimations of the hawk that Maryam will be when she is her mother's age. Maryam now has a gently aquiline face—''the sweep of the sword of love''—Chib has called that nose. Bold but beautiful. However, her mother does look like a dirty old eagle. And her aunt—uneaglish but something of the camel in those features.

Chib suppresses the unfavorable, even treacherous, comparisons. But he cannot suppress the three bearded, robed, and unwashed men who gather around him.

Chib smiles but says, "I don't remember inviting you."

They look blank since rapidly spoken LA English is a huftymagufty to them. Abu—generic name for any Egyptian in Beverly Hills—rasps an oath so ancient even the pre-Mohammed Meccans knew it. He forms a fist. Another Arab steps towards the painting and draws back a foot as if to kick it.

At this moment, Maryam's mother discovers that it is as dangerous to stand in a canoe as on a camel. It is worse, because the three women cannot swim.

Neither can the middle-aged Arab who attacks Chib, only to find his victim sidestepping and then urging him on into the lake with a foot in the rear. One of the young men rushes Chib; the other starts to kick at the painting. Both halt on hearing the three women scream and on seeing them go over into the water.

Then the two run to the edge of the lake, where they also go into the water, propelled by one of Chib's hands in each of their backs. A bolgan hears the six of them screaming and thrashing around and runs over to Chib. Chib is becoming concerned because Maryam is having trouble staying above the water. Her terror is not faked.

What Chib does not understand is why they are all carrying on so. Their feet must be on the bottom; the surface is below their chins. Despite which, Maryam looks as if she is going to drown. So do the others, but he is not interested in them. He should go in after Maryam. However, if he does, he will have to get a change of clothes before going to the showing.

At this thought, he laughs loudly and then even more loudly as the bolgan goes in after the women. He picks up the painting and walks off laughing. Before he reaches the Center, he sobers.

"Now, how come Grandpa was so right? How does he read me so well? Am I fickle, too shallow? No, I have been too deeply in love too many times. Can I help it if I love Beauty, and the beauties I love do not have enough Beauty? My eye is too demanding; it cancels the urgings of my heart.''

THE MASSACRE OF THE INNER SENSE

The entrance hall (one of twelve) which Chib enters was designed by Grandpa Winnegan. The visitor comes into a long curving tube lined with mirrors at various angles. He sees a triangular door at the end of the corridor. The door seems to be too tiny for anybody over nine years old to enter. The illusion makes the visitor feel as if he's walking up the wall as he progresses towards the door. At the end of the tube, the visitor is convinced he's standing on the ceiling.

But the door gets larger as he approaches until it becomes huge. Commentators have guessed that this entrance is the architect's symbolic representation of the gateway to the world of art. One should stand on his head before entering the wonderland of aesthetics.

On going in, the visitor thinks at first that the tremendous room is inside out or reversed. He gets even dizzier. The far wall actually seems the near wall until the visitor gets reorientated. Some people can't adjust and have to get out before they faint or vomit.

On the right hand is a hatrack with a sign: HANG YOUR HEAD HERE. A double pun by Grandpa, who always carries a joke too far for most people. If Grandpa goes beyond the bounds of verbal good taste, his great-great-grandson has overshot the moon in his paintings. Thirty of his latest have been revealed, including the last three of his Dog Series: *Dog Star, Dog Would* and *Dog Tiered*. Ruskinson and his disciples are threatening to throw up. Luscus and his flock praise, but they're restrained. Luscus has told them to wait until he talks to young Winnegan before they go all-out. The fido men are busy shooting and interviewing both and trying to provoke a quarrel.

The main room of the building is a huge hemisphere with a bright ceiling which runs through the complete spectrum every nine minutes. The floor is a giant chessboard, and in the center of each square is a face, each of a great in the various arts. Michelangelo, Mozart, Balzac, Zeuxis, Beethoven, Li Po, Twain, Dostoyevsky, Farmisto, Mbuzi, Cupel, Krishnagurti, etc. Ten squares are left faceless so that future generations may add their own nominees for immortality.

The lower part of the wall is painted with murals depicting significant events in the lives of the artists. Against the curving wall are nine stages, one for each of the Muses. On a console above each stage is a giant statue of the presiding goddess. They are naked and have overripe figures: huge-breasted, broad-hipped, sturdy-legged, as if the sculptor thought of them as Earth goddesses, not refined intellectual types.

The faces are basically structured like the smooth placid faces of classical Greek statues, but they have an unsettling expression around the mouths and eyes. The lips are smiling but seem ready to break into a snarl. The eyes are deep and menacing. DON'T SELL ME OUT, they say. IF YOU DO . . .

A transparent plastic hemisphere extends over each stage and has acoustic properties which keep people who are not beneath the shell from hearing the sounds emanating from the stage and vice versa.

Chib makes his way through the noisy crowd towards the stage of Polyhymnia, the Muse who includes painting in her province. He passes the stage on which Benedictine is standing and pouring her lead heart out in an alchemy of golden notes. She sees Chib and manages somehow to glare at him and at the same time to keep smiling at her audience. Chib ignores her but observes that she has replaced the dress ripped in the tavern. He sees also the many policemen stationed around the building. The crowd does not seem in an explosive mood. Indeed, it seems happy, if boisterous. But the police know how deceptive this can be. One spark . . .

Chib goes by the stage of Calliope, where Omar Runic is extemporizing. He comes to Polyhymnia's, nods at Rex Luscus, who waves at him, and sets his painting on the stage. It is titled *The Massacre of the Innocents* (subtitle: *Dog in the Manger*).

The painting depicts a stable.

The stable is a grotto with curiously shaped stalactites. The light that breaks—or fractures—through the cave is Chib's red. It penetrates every object, doubles its strength, and then rays out jaggedly. The viewer, moving from side to side to get a complete look, can actually see the many levels of light as he moves, and thus he catches glimpses of the figures under the exterior figures.

The cows, sheep, and horses are in stalls at the end of the cave. Some are looking with horror at Mary and the infant. Others have their mouths open, evidently trying to warn Mary. Chib has used the legend that the animals in the manager were able to talk to each other the night Christ was born.

Joseph, a tired old man, so slumped he seems backboneless, is in a corner. He wears two horns, but each has a halo, so it's all right.

Mary's back is to the bed of straw on which the infant is supposed to be. From a trapdoor in the floor of the cave, a man is reaching to place a huge egg on the straw bed. He is in a cave beneath the cave and is dressed in modern clothes, has a boozy expression, and, like Joseph, slumps as if invertebrate. Behind him a grossly fat woman, looking remarkably like Chib's mother, has the baby, which the man passed on to her before putting the foundling egg on the straw bed.

The baby has an exquisitely beautiful face and is suffused with a white glow from his halo. The woman has removed the halo from his head and is using the sharp edge to butcher the baby.

Chib has a deep knowledge of anatomy, since he has dissected many corpses while getting his Ph.D. in art at Beverly Hills U. The body of the infant is not unnaturally elongated, as so many of Chib's figures are. It is more than photographic; it seems to be an actual baby. Its viscera is unraveled through a large bloody hole.

The onlookers are struck in their viscera as if this were not a painting but a real infant, slashed and disemboweled, found on their doorsteps as they left home.

The egg has a semitransparent shell. In its murky yolk floats a hideous little devil, horns, hooves, tail. Its blurred features resemble a combination of Henry Ford's and Uncle Sam's. When the viewers shift to one side or the other, the faces of others appear: prominents in the development of modern society.

The window is crowded with wild animals that have come to adore but have stayed to scream soundlessly in horror. The beasts in the foreground are those that have been exterminated by man or survive only in zoos and natural preserves. The dodo, the blue whale, the passenger pigeon, the quagga, the gorilla, orangutan, polar bear, cougar, lion, tiger, grizzly bear, California condor, kangaroo, wombat, rhinoceros, bald eagle.

Behind them are other animals and, on a hill, the dark crouching shapes of the Tasmanian aborigine and Haitian Indian.

"What is your considered opinion of this rather remarkable painting, Doctor Luscus?'' a fido interviewer asks.

Luscus smiles and says, "I'll have a considered judgment in a few minutes. Perhaps you'd better talk to Doctor Ruskinson first. He seems to have made up his mind at once. Fools and angels, you know.''

Ruskinson's red face and scream of fury are transmitted over the fido.

"The shit heard around the world!" Chib says loudly.

"INSULT! SPITTLE! PLASTIC DUNG! A BLOW IN THE FACE OF ART AND A KICK IN THE BUTT FOR HUMANITY! INSULT! INSULT!"

"Why is it such an insult, Doctor Ruskinson?" the fido man says. "Because it mocks the Christian faith, and also the Panamorite faith? It doesn't seem to me it does that. It seems to me that Winnegan is trying to say that men have perverted Christianity, maybe all religions, all ideals, for their own greedy self-destructive purposes, that man is basically a killer and a perverter. At least, that's what I get out of it, although of course I'm only a simple layman, and . . .''

"Let the critics make the analysis, young man!" Ruskinson snaps. "Do you have a double Ph.D., one in psychiatry and one in art? Have you been certified as a critic by the government?

"Winnegan, who has no talent whatsoever, let alone this genius that various self-deluded blowhards prate about, this abomination from Beverly Hills, presents his junk—actually a mishmash which has attracted attention solely because of a new technique that any electronic technician could invent—I am enraged that a mere gimmick, a trifling novelty, can not only fool certain sectors of the public but highly educated and federally certified critics such as Doctor Luscus here—although there will always be scholarly asses who bray so loudly, pompously, and obscurely that . . .''

"Isn't it true," the fido man says, "that many painters
we now call great, Van Gogh for one, were condemned
or ignored by their contemporary critics? And . . ."

The fido man, skilled in provoking anger for the benefit of his viewers, pauses. Ruskinson swells, his head a
bloodvessel just before aneurysm.

"I'm no ignorant layman!" he screams. "I can't help
it that there have been Luscuses in the past! I know what
I'm talking about! Winnegan is only a micrometeorite in
the heaven of Art, not fit to shine the shoes of the great
luminaries of painting. His reputation has been pumped
up by a certain clique so it can shine in the reflected
glory, the hyenas, biting the hand that feeds them, like
mad dogs . . ."

"Aren't you mixing your metaphors a little bit?" the
fido man says.

Luscus takes Chib's hand tenderly and draws him to
one side where they're out of fido range.

"Darling Chib," he coos, "now is the time to declare
yourself. You know how vastly I love you, not only as
an artist but for yourself. It must be impossible for you
to resist any longer the deeply sympathetic vibrations that
leap unhindered between us. God, if you only knew how
I dreamed of you, my glorious godlike Chib, with . . ."

"If you think I'm going to say yes because you have
the power to make or break my reputation, to deny me
the grant, you're wrong," Chib says. He jerks his hand
away.

Luscus' good eye glares. He says, "Do you find me
repulsive? Surely it can't be on moral grounds . . ."

"It's the principle of the thing," Chib says. "Even if
I were in love with you, which I'm not, I wouldn't let
you make love to me. I want to be judged on my merit
alone, that only. Come to think of it, I don't give a damn
about anybody's judgment. I don't want to hear praise or
blame from you or anybody. Look at my paintings and

talk to each other, you jackals. But don't try to make me agree with your little images of me.''

THE ONLY GOOD CRITIC
IS A DEAD CRITIC

Omar Runic has left his dais and now stands before Chib's paintings. He places one hand on his naked left chest, on which is tattooed the face of Herman Melville, Homer occupying the other place of honor on his right breast. He shouts loudly, his black eyes like furnace doors blown out by explosion. As has happened before, he is seized with inspiration derived from Chib's paintings.

''Call me Ahab, not Ishmael.
  For I have hooked the Leviathan.
  I am the wild ass's colt born to a man.
  Lo, my eye has seen it all!
  My bosom is like wine that has no vent.
  I am a sea with doors, but the doors are stuck.
  Watch out! The skin will burst; the doors will break.

''You are Nimrod, I say to my friend, Chib.
  And now is the hour when God says to his angels,
  If this is what he can do as a beginning, then
  Nothing is impossible for him.
  He will be blowing his horn before
  The ramparts of Heaven and shouting for
  The Moon as hostage, the Virgin as wife,
  And demanding a cut on the profits
  From the Great Whore of Babylon.''

"Stop that son of a bitch!" the Festival Director shouts. "He'll cause a riot like he did last year!"

The bolgani begin to move in. Chib watches Luscus, who is talking to the fido man. Chib can't hear Luscus, but he's sure Luscus is not saying complimentary things about him.

"Melville wrote of me long before I was born.
  I'm the man who wants to comprehend
  The Universe but comprehend on my terms.
  I am Ahab whose hate must pierce, shatter,
  All impediment of Time, Space, or Subject
  Mortality and hurl my fierce
  Incandescence into the Womb of Creation,
  Disturbing in its Lair whatever Force or
  Unknown Thing-in-Itself crouches there,
  Remote, removed, unrevealed."

The Director gestures at the police to remove Runic. Ruskinson is still shouting, although the cameras are pointing at Runic or Luscus. One of the Young Radishes, Huga Wells-Erb Heinsturbury, the science-fiction author-ess, is shaking with hysteria generated by Runic's voice and with a lust for revenge. She is sneaking up on a *Time* fido man. *Time* had long ago ceased to be a magazine, since there are no magazines, but became a government-supported communications bureau. *Time* is an example of Uncle Sam's left-hand, right-hand, hands-off policy of providing communications bureaus with all they need and at the same time permitting the bureau executives to de-termine the bureau policies. Thus, government provision and free speech are united. This is fine, in theory, any-way.

Time has revived several of its original policies, that is, truth and objectivity must be sacrificed for the sake of a witticism and science-fiction must be put down. *Time* has sneered at every one of Heinsturbury's works, and so she is out to get some personal satisfaction for the hurt caused by the unfair reviews.

> *"Quid nunc? Cui bono?*
> Time? Space? Substance? Accident?
> When you die—Hell? Nirvana?
> Nothing is nothing to think about.
> The canons of philosophy boom.
> Their projectiles are duds.
> The ammo heaps of theology blow up,
> Set off by the saboteur Reason.
>
> "Call me Ephraim, for I was halted
> At the Ford of God and could not tongue
> The sibilance to let me pass.
> Well, I can't pronounce shibboleth,
> But I can say shit!"

Huga Wells-Erb Heinsturbury kicks the *Time* fido man in the balls. He throws up his hands, and the football-shaped, football-sized camera sails from his hands and strikes a youth on the head. The youth is a Young Radish, Ludwig Euterpe Mahlzart. He is smoldering with rage because of the damnation of his tone poem, *Jetting The Stuff Of Future Hells*, and the camera is the extra fuel needed to make him blaze up uncontrollably. He punches the chief musical critic in his fat belly.

Huga, not the *Time* man, is screaming with pain. Her bare toes have struck the hard plastic armor with which the *Time* man, recipient of many such a kick, protects his genitals. Huga hops around on one foot while holding the injured foot in her hands. She twirls into a girl, and there is a chain effect. A man falls against the *Time* man, who is stooping over to pick up his camera.

"Ahaaa!" Huga screams and tears off the *Time* man's

helmet and straddles him and beats him over the head
with the optical end of the camera. Since the solid-state
camera is still working, it is sending to billions of viewers some very intriguing, if dizzying, pictures. Blood
obscures one side of the picture, but not so much that
the viewers are wholly cheated. And then they get another novel shot as the camera flies into the air again,
turning over and over.

A bolgan has shoved his shock-stick against her back,
causing her to stiffen and propel the camera in a high arc
behind her. Huga's current lover grapples with the bolgan; they roll on the floor; a Westwood juvenile picks up
the shock-stick and has a fine time goosing the adults
around him until a local youth jumps him.

"Riots are the opium of the people," the Police Chief
groans. He calls in all units and puts in a call to the Chief
of Police of Westwood, who is, however, having his own
troubles.

Runic beats his breast and howls.

> "Sir, I exist! And don't tell me,
>   As you did Crane, that that creates
>   No obligation in you towards me.
>   I am a man; I am unique.
>   I've thrown the Bread out the window,
>   Pissed in the Wine, pulled the plug
>   From the bottom of the Ark, cut the Tree
>   For firewood, and if there were a Holy
>   Ghost, I'd goose him.
>   But I know that it all does not mean
>   A God damned thing.
>   That nothing means nothing,
>   That is is is and not-is not is is-not
>   That a rose is a rose is a
>   That we are here and will not be
>   And that is all we can know!"

Ruskinson sees Chib coming towards him, squawks, and tries to escape. Chib seizes the canvas of *Dogmas from a Dog* and batters Ruskinson over the head with it. Luscus protests in horror, not because of the damage done to Ruskinson but because the painting might be damaged. Chib turns around and batters Luscus in the stomach with the oval's edge.

"The earth lurches like a ship going down,
Its back almost broken by the flood of
Excrement from the heavens and the deeps,
What God in His terrible munificence
Has granted on hearing Ahab cry,
Bullshit! Bullshit!

"I weep to think that this is Man
And this his end. But wait!
On the crest of the flood, a three-master
Of antique shape. The Flying Dutchman!
And Ahab is astride a ship's deck once more.
Laugh, you Fates, and mock, you Norns!
For I am Ahab and I am Man,
And though I cannot break a hole
through the wall of What Seems
To grab a handful of What Is,
Yet, I will keep on punching.
And I and my crew will not give up,
Though the timbers split beneath our feet
And we sink to become indistinguishable
From the general excrement.

"For a moment that will burn on the
Eye of God forever, Ahab stands
Outlined against the blaze of Orion,
Fist clenched, a bloody phallus,
Like Zeus exhibiting the trophy of
The unmanning of his father Cronus.

And then he and his crew and ship
Dip and hurtle headlong over
The edge of the world.
And from what I hear, they are still

F
a
l
l
i
n
g"

Chib is shocked into a quivering mass by a jolt from a bolgan's electrical riot stick. While he is recovering, he hears his Grandpa's voice issuing from the transceiver in his hat.

"Chib, come quick! Accipiter has broken in and is trying to get through the door of my room!"

Chib gets up and fights and shoves his way to the exit. When he arrives, panting, at his home he finds that the door to Grandpa's room has been opened. The IRB men and electronic technicians are standing in the hallway. Chib bursts into Grandpa's room. Accipiter is standing in its middle and quivering and pale. Nervous stone. He sees Chib and shrinks back, saying, "It wasn't my fault. I had to break in. It was the only way I could find out for sure. It wasn't my fault; I didn't touch him."

Chib's throat is closing in on itself. He cannot speak. He kneels down and takes Grandpa's hand. Grandpa has a slight smile on his blue lips. Once and for all, he has eluded Accipiter. In his hand is the latest sheet of his Ms.:

THROUGH BALAKLAVAS OF HATE,
THEY CHARGE TOWARDS GOD

For most of my life, I have seen only a truly devout few and a great majority of truly indifferent. But there is a new spirit abroad. So many young men and women have revived, not a love for God, but a violent antipathy towards Him. This excites and restores me. Youths like my grandson and Runic shout blasphemies and so worship Him. If they did not believe, they would never think about Him. I now have some confidence in the future.

TO THE STICKS VIA THE STYX

Dressed in black, Chib and his mother go down the tube entrance to level 13B. It's luminous-walled, spacious, and the fare is free. Chib tells the ticket-fido his destination. Behind the wall, the protein computer, no larger than a human brain, calculates. A coded ticket slides out of a slot. Chib takes the ticket, and they go to the bay, a great incurve, where he sticks the ticket into a slot. Another ticket protrudes, and a mechanical voice repeats the information on the ticket in World and LA English, in case they can't read.

Gondolas shoot into the bay and decelerate to a stop. Wheelless, they float in a continually rebalancing graviton field. Sections of the bay slide back to make ports for the gondolas. Passengers step into the cages designated for them. The cages move forward; their doors open automatically. The passengers step into the gondolas. They sit down and wait while the safety meshmold closes over them. From the recess of the chassis, transparent plastic curves rise and meet to form a dome.

Automatically timed, monitored by redundant protein computers for safety, the gondolas wait until the coast is clear. On receiving the go-ahead, they move slowly out of the bay to the tube. They pause while getting another affirmation, trebly checked in microseconds. Then they move swiftly into the tube.

Whoosh! Whoosh! Other gondolas pass them. The tube glows yellowly as if filled with electrified gas. The gondola accelerates rapidly. A few are still passing it, but Chib's speeds up and soon none can catch up with it. The round posterior of a gondola ahead is a glimmering quarry that will not be caught until it slows before mooring at its destined bay. There are not many gondolas in the tube. Despite a 100-million population, there is little traffic on the north-south route. Most LAers stay in the self-sufficient walls of their clutches. There is more traffic on the east-west tubes, since a small percentage prefer the public ocean beaches to the municipality swimming pools.

The vehicle screams southward. After a few minutes, the tube begins to slope down, and suddenly it is at a 45-degree angle to the horizontal. They flash by level after level.

Through the transparent walls, Chib glimpses the people and architecture of other cities. Level 8, Long Beach, is interesting. Its homes look like two cut-quartz pie plates, one on top of another, open end on open end, and the unit mounted on a column of carved figures, the exit-entrance ramp a flying buttress.

At level 3A, the tube straightens out. Now the gondola races past establishments the sight of which causes Mama to shut her eyes. Chib squeezes his mother's hand and thinks of the half-brother and cousin who are behind the yellowish plastic. This level contains fifteen percent of the population, the retarded, the incurable insane, the too-ugly, the monstrous, the senile aged. They swarm here, the vacant or twisted faces pressed against the tube wall to watch the pretty cars float by.

"Humanitarian" medical science keeps alive the babies that *should*—by Nature's imperative—have died. Ever since the 20th century, humans with defective genes have been saved from death. Hence, the continual spreading of these genes. The tragic thing is that science can now detect and correct defective genes in the ovum and sperm. Theoretically, all human beings could be blessed with totally healthy bodies and physically perfect brains. But the rub is that we don't have near enough doctors and facilities to keep up with the births. This despite the ever decreasing drop in the birth rate.

Medical science keeps people living so long that senility strikes. So, more and more slobbering mindless decrepits. And also an accelerating addition of the mentally addled. There are therapies and drugs to restore most of them to "normalcy," but not enough doctors and facilities. Some day there may be, but that doesn't help the contemporary unfortunate.

What to do now? The ancient Greeks placed defective babies in the fields to die. The Eskimos shipped out their old people on ice floes. Should we gas our abnormal infants and seniles? Sometimes, I think it's the merciful thing to do. But I can't ask somebody else to pull the switch when I won't.

I would shoot the first man to reach for it.

—from Grandpa's *Private Ejaculations*

The gondola approaches one of the rare intersections. Its passengers see down the broad-mouthed tube to their right. An express flies towards them; it looms. Collision course. They know better, but they can't keep from gripping the mesh, gritting their teeth, and bracing their legs. Mama gives a small shriek. The flier hurtles over them and disappears, the flapping scream of air a soul on its way to underworld judgment.

The tube dips again until it levels out on 1. They see the round below and the massive self-adjusting pillars supporting the megalopolis. They whiz by over a little town, quaint, early 21st century LA preserved as a museum, one of many beneath the cube.

Fifteen minutes after embarking, the Winnegans reach the end of the line. An elevator takes them to the ground, where they enter a big black limousine. This is furnished by a private-enterprise mortuary, since Uncle Sam or the LA government will pay for cremation but not for burial. The Church no longer insists on interment, leaving it to the religionists to choose between being wind-blown ashes or underground corpses.

The sun is halfway towards the zenith. Mama begins to have trouble breathing and her arms and neck redden and swell. The three times she's been outside the walls, she's been attacked with this allergy despite the air conditioning of the limousine. Chib pats her hand while they're riding over a roughly patched road. The archaic eighty-year-old, fuel-cell-powered, electric-motor-driven vehicle is, however, rough-riding only by comparison with the gondola. It covers the ten kilometers to the cemetery speedily, stopping once to let deer cross the road.

Father Fellini greets them. He is distressed because he is forced to tell them that the Church feels that Grandpa has committed sacrilege. To substitute another man's body for his corpse, to have mass said over it, to have it buried in sacred ground is to blaspheme. Moreover,

Grandpa died an unrepentant criminal. At least, to the knowledge of the Church, he made no contrition just before he died.

Chib expects this refusal. St. Mary's of BH-14 has declined to perform services for Grandpa within its walls. But Grandpa has often told Chib that he wants to be buried beside his ancestors, and Chib is determined that Grandpa will get his wish.

Chib says, "I'll bury him myself! Right on the edge of the graveyard!"

"You can't do that!" the priest, mortuary officials, and a federal agent say simultaneously.

"The Hell I can't! Where's the shovel?"

It is then that he sees the thin dark face and falciform nose of Accipiter. The agent is supervising the digging up of Grandpa's (first) coffin. Nearby are at least fifty fido men shooting with their minicameras, the transceivers floating a few decameters near them. Grandpa is getting full coverage, as befits the Last Of The Billionaires and The Greatest Criminal Of The Century.

Fido interviewer: "Mr. Accipiter, could we have a few words from you? I'm not exaggerating when I say that there are probably at least ten billion people watching this historic event. After all, even the grade-school kids know of Win-again Winnegan.

"How do you feel about this? You've been on the case for 26 years. The successful conclusion must give you great satisfaction."

Accipiter, unsmiling as the essence of diorite: "Well, actually, I've not devoted full time to this case. Only about three years of accumulative time. But since I've spent at least several days each month on it, you might say I've been on Winnegan's trail for 26 years."

Interviewer: "It's been said that the ending of this case also means the end of the IRB. If we've not been misinformed, the IRB was only kept functioning because of

Winnegan. You had other business, of course, during this time, but the tracking down of counterfeiters and gamblers who don't report their income has been turned over to other bureaus. Is this true? If so, what do you plan to do?''

Accipiter, voice flashing a crystal of emotion: ''Yes, the IRB is being disbanded. But not until after the case against Winnegan's grand-daughter and her son is finished. They harbored him and are, therefore, accessories after the fact.

''In fact, almost the entire population of Beverly Hills, level 14, should be on trial. I know, but can't prove it as yet, that everybody, including the municipal Chief of Police, was well aware that Winnegan was hiding in that house. Even Winnegan's priest knew it, since Winnegan frequently went to mass and to confession. His priest claims that he urged Winnegan to turn himself in and also refused to give him absolution unless he did so.

''But Winnegan, a hardened 'mouse'—I mean, criminal, if ever I saw one, refused to follow the priest's urgings. He claimed that he had not committed a crime, that, believe it or not, Uncle Sam was the criminal. Imagine the effrontery, the depravity, of the man!''

Interviewer: ''Surely you don't plan to arrest the entire population of Beverly Hills 14?''

Accipiter: ''I have been advised not to.''

Interviewer: ''Do you plan on retiring after this case is wound up?''

Accipiter: ''No. I intend to transfer to the Greater LA Homicide Bureau. Murder for profit hardly exists any more, but there are still crimes of passion, thank God!''

Interviewer: ''Of course, if young Winnegan should win his case against you—he has charged you with invasion of domestic privacy, illegal housebreaking, and directly causing his great-great-grandfather's death—then

208

you won't be able to work for the Homicide Bureau or any police department."

Accipiter, flashing several crystals of emotion: "It's no wonder we law enforcers have such a hard time operating effectively! Sometimes, not only the majority of citizens seem to be on the law-breaker's side but my own employers . . ."

Interviewer: "Would you care to complete that statement? I'm sure your employers are watching this channel. No? I understand that Winnegan's trial and yours are, for some reason, scheduled to take place *at the same time*. How do you plan to be present at both trials? Heh, heh! Some fido-casters are calling you The Simultaneous Man!"

Accipiter, face darkening: "Some idiot clerk did that! He incorrectly fed the data into the legal computer. And he, or somebody, turned off the error-override circuit, and the computer burned up. The clerk is suspected of deliberately making the error—by me anyway, and let the idiot sue me if he wishes—anyway, there have been too many cases like this, and . . ."

Interviewer: "Would you mind summing up the course of this case for our viewers' benefit? Just the highlights, please."

Accipiter: "Well, ah, as you know, fifty years ago all large private-enterprise businesses had become government bureaus. All except the building construction firm, the Finnegan Fifty-three States Company, of which the president was Finn Finnegan. He was the father of the man who is to be buried—somewhere—today.

"Also, all unions except the largest, the construction union, were dissolved or were government unions. Actually, the company and its union were one, because all employees got ninety-five per cent of the money, distributed more or less equally among them. Old Finnegan

209

was both the company president and union business agent-secretary.

"By hook or crook, mainly by crook, I believe, the firm-union had resisted the inevitable absorption. There were investigations into Finnegan's methods: coercion and blackmail of U.S. Senators and even U.S. Supreme Court Justices. Nothing was, however, proved."

Interviewer: "For the benefit of our viewers who may be a little hazy on their history, even fifty years ago money was used only for the purchase of nonguaranteed items. Its other use, as today, was as an index of prestige and social esteem. At one time, the government was thinking of getting rid of currency entirely, but a study revealed that it had great psychological value. The income tax was also kept, although the government had no use for money, because the size of a man's tax determined prestige and also because it enabled the government to remove a large amount of currency from circulation."

Accipiter: "Anyway, when old Finnegan died, the federal government renewed its pressure to incorporate the construction workers and the company officials as civil servants. But young Finnegan proved to be as foxy and vicious as his old man. I don't suggest, of course, that the fact that his uncle was President of the U.S. at that time had anything to do with young Finnegan's success."

Interviewer: "Young Finnegan was seventy years old when his father died."

Accipiter: "During this struggle, which went on for many years, Finnegan decided to rename himself Winnegan. It's a pun on Win Again. He seems to have had a childish, even imbecilic, delight in puns, which, frankly, I don't understand. Puns, I mean."

Interviewer: "For the benefit of our non-American viewers, who may not know of our national custom of Naming Day . . . this was originated by the Panamorites.

When a citizen comes of age, he may at any time thereafter take a new name, one which he believes to be appropriate to his temperament or goal in life. I might point out that Uncle Sam, who's been unfairly accused of trying to impose conformity upon his citizen's, encourages this individualistic approach to life. This despite the increased record-keeping required on the government's part.

"I might also point out something else of interest. The government claimed that Grandpa Winnegan was mentally incompetent. My listeners will pardon me, I hope, if I take up a moment of your time to explain the basis of Uncle Sam's assertion. Now, for the benefit of those among you who are unacquainted with an early 20th-century classic, *Finnegan's Wake*, despite your government's wish for you to have a free lifelong education, the author, James Joyce, derived the title from an old vaudeville song."

(Half-fadeout while a monitor briefly explains "vaudeville.")

"The song was about Tim Finnegan, an Irish hod carrier who fell off a ladder while drunk and was supposedly killed. During the Irish wake held for Finnegan, the corpse is accidentally splashed with whiskey. Finnegan, feeling the touch of the whiskey, the 'water of life,' sits up in his coffin and then climbs out to drink and dance with the mourners.

"Grandpa Winnegan always claimed that the vaudeville song was based on reality, you can't keep a good man down, and that the original Tim Finnegan was his ancestor. This preposterous statement was used by the government in its suit against Winnegan.

"However, Winnegan produced documents to substantiate his assertion. Later—too late—the documents were proved to be forgeries."

Accipiter: "The government's case against Winnegan

was strengthened by the rank and file's sympathy with the government. Citizens were complaining that the business-union was undemocratic and discriminatory. The officials and workers were getting relatively high wages, but many citizens had to be contented with their guaranteed income. So, Winnegan was brought to trial and accused, justly, of course, of various crimes, among which were subversion of democracy.

"Seeing the inevitable, Winnegan capped his criminal career. He somehow managed to steal 20 billion dollars from the federal deposit vault. This sum, by the way, was equal to half the currency then existing in Greater LA. Winnegan disappeared with the money, which he had not only stolen but had not paid income tax on. Unforgivable. I don't know why so many people have glamorized this villain's feat. Why, I've even seen fido shows with him as the hero, thinly disguised under another name, of course."

Interviewer: "Yes, folks, Winnegan committed the Crime Of The Age. And, although he has finally been located, and is to be buried today—somewhere—the case is not completely closed. The federal government says it is. But where is the money, the 20 billion dollars?"

Accipiter: "Actually, the money has no value now except as collector's items. Shortly after the theft, the government called in all currency and then issued new bills that could not be mistaken for the old. The government had been wanting to do something like this for a long time, anyway, because it believed that there was too much currency, and it only reissued half the amount taken in.

"I'd like very much to know where the money is. I won't rest until I do. I'll hunt it down if I have to do it on my own time."

Interviewer: "You may have plenty of time to do that if young Winnegan wins his case. Well, folks, as most of you may know, Winnegan was found dead in a lower level of San Francisco about a year after he disappeared. His grand-daughter identified the body, and the finger-prints, earprints, retinaprints, teethprints, blood-type, hair-type, and a dozen other identity prints matched out.''

Chib, who has been listening, thinks that Grandpa must have spent several millions of the stolen money arranging this. He does not know, but he suspects that a research lab somewhere in the world grew the duplicate in a biotank.

This happened two years after Chib was born. When Chib was five, his grandpa showed up. Without letting Mama know he was back, he moved in. Only Chib was his confidant. It was, of course, impossible for Grandpa to go completely unnoticed by Mama, yet she now insisted that she had never seen him. Chib thought that this was to avoid prosecution for being an accessory after the crime. He was not sure. Perhaps she had blocked off his ''visitations'' from the rest of her mind. For her it would be easy, since she never knew whether today was Tuesday or Thursday and could not tell you what year it was.

Chib ignores the mortuarians, who want to know what to do with the body. He walks over to the grave. The top of the ovoid coffin is visible now, with the long elephant-like snout of the digging machine sonically crumbling the dirt and then sucking it up. Accipiter, breaking through his lifelong control, is smiling at the fidomen and rubbing his hands.

''Dance a little, you son of a bitch,'' Chib says, his anger the only block to the tears and wail building up in him.

The area around the coffin is cleared to make room for the grappling arms of the machine. These descend, hook under, and lift the black, irradiated-plastic, mocksilver-arabesqued coffin up and out onto the grass. Chib, seeing the IRB men begin to open the coffin, starts to say something but closes his mouth. He watches intently, his knees bent as if getting ready to jump. The fidomen close in, their eyeball-shaped cameras pointing at the group around the coffin.

Groaning, the lid rises. There is a big bang. Dense dark smoke billows. Accipiter and his men, blackened, eyes wide and white, coughing, stagger out of the cloud. The fidomen are running every which way or stooping to pick up their cameras. Those who were standing far enough back can see that the explosion took place at the bottom of the grave. Only Chib knows that the raising of the coffin lid has activated the detonating device in the grave.

He is also the first to look up into the sky at the projectile soaring from the grave because only he expected it. The rocket climbs up to five hundred feet while the fidomen train their cameras on it. It bursts apart and from it a ribbon unfolds between two round objects. The objects expand to become balloons while the ribbon becomes a huge banner.

On it, in big black letters, are the words

WINNEGAN'S FAKE!

Twenty billions of dollars buried beneath the supposed bottom of the grave burn furiously. Some bills, blown up in the geyser of fireworks, are carried by the wind while IRB men, fidomen, mortuary officials, and municipality officials chase them.

Mama is stunned.

Accipiter looks as if he is having a stroke.

Chib cries and then laughs and rolls on the ground.

Grandpa has again screwed Uncle Sam and has also pulled his greatest pun where all the world can see it.

"Oh, you old man!" Chib sobs between laughing fits. "Oh, you old man! How I love you!"

While he is rolling on the ground again, roaring so hard his ribs hurt, he feels a paper in his hand. He stops and gets on his knees and calls after the man who gave it to him. The man says, "I was paid by your grandfather to hand it to you when he was buried."

Chib reads.

I hope nobody was hurt, not even the IRB men.

Final advice from the Wise Old Man In The Cave. Tear loose. Leave LA. Leave the country. Go to Egypt. Let your mother ride the purple wage on her own. She can do it if she practices thrift and self-denial. If she can't, that's not your fault.

You are fortunate indeed to have been born with talent, if not genius, and to be strong enough to want to rip out the umbilical cord. So do it. Go to Egypt. Steep yourself in the ancient culture. Stand before the Sphinx. Ask her (actually, it's a he) the Question.

Then visit one of the zoological preserves south of the Nile. Live for a while in a reasonable facsimile of Nature as she was before mankind dishonored and disfigured her. There, where Homo Sapiens (?) evolved from the killer ape, absorb the spirit of that ancient place and time.

You've been painting with your penis, which I'm afraid was more stiffened with bile than with passion for life. Learn to paint with your heart. Only thus will you become great and true.

Paint.

Then, go wherever you want to go. I'll be with

you as long as you're alive to remember me. To quote Runic, "I'll be the Northern Lights of your soul."

Hold fast to the belief that there will be others to love you just as much as I did or even more. What is more important, you must love them as much as they love you.

Can you do this?

SCIENCE FICTION FROM
PHILIP JOSE FARMER

☐ 53555-6 THE CACHE $2.95
☐   Canada $3.95

☐ 50889-0 DAYWORLD BREAKUP $4.95
☐   Canada $5.95

☐ 54757-2 THE OTHER LOG OF PHILEAS FOGG $3.50
☐   Canada $4.50

☐ 53773-4 STATIONS OF THE NIGHTMARE $3.95
☐   Canada $4.95

☐ 53764-5 TIME'S LAST GIFT $2.95
☐   Canada $3.50

THE BEST IN
SCIENCE FICTION

Buy them at your local bookstore or use this handy coupon:
Clip and mail this page with your order.

Publishers Book and Audio Mailing Service
P.O. Box 120159, Staten Island, NY 10312-0004

Please send me the book(s) I have checked above. I am enclosing $ _____
(Please add $1.25 for the first book, and $.25 for each additional book to cover postage and handling.
Send check or money order only—no CODs.)

Name _____
Address _____
City _____ State/Zip _____
Please allow six weeks for delivery. Prices subject to change without notice.